Masquerade in Venice

Masquerade in Venice

VELDA JOHNSTON

A Novel of Suspense

DODD, MEAD & COMPANY
NEW YORK

Printed in the United States of America

For my niece, Sharon Seymour

CHAPTER 1

IT IS EASY to see why the Venice police thought I might be responsible for that death in the Belzonis' crumbling but proud old house. First of all, I was a stranger, an American spinster of almost twenty-four, who had arrived alone in a country where no well-born woman travels without the protection of a husband or servants. What was even more damning, I had left my native New England under the sort of circumstances often referred to as a cloud.

Yes, galling as those unjust suspicions were, I could understand them. I'd had to admit to a coroner's jury that my negligence had been partially responsible for the death of that old woman back in Connecticut. So why shouldn't official suspicion fall upon me after that sudden death beneath the Belzonis' ancient roof?

Until the night of my arrival in Venice, I had never met my aged kinswoman, the Contessa Belzoni, or her beautiful granddaughter or her younger grandson. I was very tired that rainy night that marked the end of my long journey. In New York, unable to find any space aboard a passenger ship except a too expensive first-class cabin, I had finally sailed on a twenty-year-old cargo ship, with limited passenger accommodations, which had first seen service in the waning days of the Civil War. Its cabins were cramped, and the deck space allotted to passengers was meager—although that had mattered little, since most of the time the weather had been too rough for the passengers to do anything but lie in their bunks watching oil wall lamps swing giddily in their gimbals. Once I reached Genoa, of course, there had been the train journey across Italy to Venice.

Now, as the Belzoni gondola carried me from the railway station along the Grand Canal, rain-blurred lanterns hanging in arched entryways afforded me only a dim impression of close-packed houses, looming tall on either side. A mist was rising from the black water, and that, combined with the chill drizzle, made me feel that the time of year was November rather than mid-May. But then, my Venetian-born grandmother had told me that Venice often seemed in an autumnal mood, like some deposed queen musing upon the days of her power and her unfaded loveliness.

The gondola angled closer to the right side of the wide, watery thoroughfare. Ahead I could see a break in the line of houses, marking the entrance to a side canal. Slowly we moved past the colonnaded façade of a tall marble house. Pulses quickening, I wondered if this could be the Ca' Belzoni. My grandmother had told me that it stood at the junction of a smaller canal with the Grand Canal. I glanced up. Yes, there above the wide arched entryway was the gigantic lion's head she had described, looking down at me with a half snarl through the rainy night.

The gondolier, standing behind me, gave a warning cry, a drawn-out "Oi-eee!" which echoed across the dark water between the tall rows of stone and masonry façades. Then, after pausing a few seconds, we turned onto the smaller canal and glided past the *palazzo's* northern wall toward a landing stage, dimly washed by light from an arched entryway beyond it. I could see a small skiff, much like the catboat my father and I used to sail on Long Island Sound, tied to one of the striped mooring poles.

Stepping from the boat, the gondolier moored it fore and aft. His name was Emilio, he had told me when he met me at the station. He was about thirty-five, a tall, muscular man in a black-and-white striped jersey and dark trousers. Despite his brawniness, he moved with the insolent grace of a big cat. Insolence lurked, too, in the smile with which he handed me onto the landing stage.

Bending, he lifted my valise from the boat. "I will take this to your room, Signorina Randall." His Italian was the sibilant Venetian sort, with "g" sounding like "z" and "c" like "x," which I myself had learned as a child from my grandmother. "Maria Rugazzi—she is our housekeeper—has told me which room it is."

I took a step toward the archway and then halted. "What's that?" I could hear a muted roaring, like that of a distant waterfall.

He smiled. "There was a bad storm farther south in the Adriatic. Now the waves are pounding at the Lido. You know of the Lido?"

"Of course." Long ago my grandmother had described to me the narrow barrier beach that shelters Venice and its sister islands of the lagoon.

"It was a bad storm. Someday in a storm the ocean will break through. Then Venice and all its people will drown." He snapped his fingers. "Like that."

As I have said, I was tired. Perhaps that was why his words conjured up for me the Adriatic's waters, roaring in a mountainous wall across the dark lagoon to engulf the city and the marble platform upon which we stood.

Then I saw the shine of enjoyment in his dark eyes. It was fun to frighten the American signorina. And he could do so with little risk. True, she was related to the family—the old Contessa's grandniece, in fact—but she was to be paid here. And that made her a servant, like himself.

I felt that I could see myself through his eyes—a young woman in a none-too-smart traveling costume of dark brown bombazine, with a too pale face, and a reticule dangling from a wrist that was far too thin, especially by Italian standards. I said coolly, "That beach has guarded Venice for a thousand years. I think it will hold a little longer."

He smiled and then moved through the archway. I followed him into a little courtyard where a willow trailed its branches onto a grassy plot and a marble bench sat against the wall. Again I looked up. I could make out, away up there beneath the fourth floor windows, dim protuberances that must be other gigantic heads my grandmother had mentioned.

Emilio had disappeared beyond a pair of doors of lacy iron grillwork. I went through them, into a marble-flagged entrance hall, in time to see him mounting a broad flight of marble stairs. I followed slowly, noticing the grotesque, naked little stone figures —were they elves?—affixed to the stairs' newel posts, and the large mural of frolicking nymphs and satyrs on the stairway wall. One of the squat little elves was rendered even less attractive by a missing nose, and the mural was cracked and even peeling in spots. I was not surprised by these signs of neglect. In New York, Carlo Belzoni—the old Contessa's grandson and therefore my second cousin—had told me with a shrug that the family fortunes, on the downgrade for the past two hundred years, were now in a depressed state indeed.

A woman in a dark, full-skirted dress had appeared at the top of the stairs. She said something to Emilio as he passed her, and then smiled down at me, inclining her head in a slight bow. It was a well-trained servant's smile, expressing no judgment. And yet I felt there was friendliness behind it, and even a touch of sympathy, although for what I could not be sure. My travel-worn appearance? The experiences that lay ahead of me as the Contessa's paid companion? Well, no matter what the Contessa's temperament, I would put up with it. I had little choice in the matter.

"Good evening," she said when I reached her. "I am Maria Rugazzi, the housekeeper." She was in her late middle years, I saw now, but still erect and vigorous-looking, with a strong-featured face and dark hair threaded with gray. "Shall I take you to the Contessa? Or would you like to go to your room first?"

I said gratefully, "My room, please."

Starched underskirts rustling, she led me toward another stairway at the opposite end of the hall. I started past an archway, and then paused. Light from oil lamps of Venetian glass flanking the archway penetrated the vast room beyond for a little distance, so that I could see a marble floor and the gleam of a huge crystal chandelier.

Maria came back to stand beside me. "That is the grand salon," she said, pride in her voice. "Many balls have been held there. Once more than a hundred years ago the brother of an English king was the honor guest, and before that an Austrian emperor."

"Are balls ever held there now?"

"Oh, yes. In late May, after Signore Carlo comes to stay with us, there is always a ball. And he will be home tomorrow, or perhaps the day after."

She turned then, and I followed her up the stairs to the landing. A portrait hung there, not some heirloom from two hundred years ago or more, but a modern painting, its colors still fresh and bright. Pausing, Maria said, "That is Signorina Isabella. It was painted six years ago when she reached twenty-one."

Isabella, my second cousin. Only she was no longer a signorina. She was married, her brother Carlo had told me, to a Venetian banker who spent most of his time traveling from one European capital to another. "She must be very beautiful," I said.

"Yes." Maria's tone was neutral. She added, with tentative warmth, "I see in you a family resemblance."

Perhaps, but a slight one. My eyes are gray, and my hair dark red. The eyes of the young woman in the portrait were green, and her hair the reddish gold that Titian loved to paint. I was naturally thin, and had grown even thinner in the past stressful months. Her arms and shoulders, revealed by a low-necked dress of green satin, were fashionably rounded.

I followed Maria up the second flight. This hall, too, was paved with marble. How chill this place was, even in May. But then, my grandmother had once told me that all the great Venetian houses were built to combat the sweltering heat of full summer.

When I asked her what Venetians did in winter, she said, "They have little china stoves carried from room to room. And they shiver a lot."

Nodding toward a closed door, Maria said, "This first room is the Contessa's." We moved on, past a row of closed doors on the left, and, on the right, a series of tall arched windows. I realized that those windows must overlook the roof of the grand salon below. At the end of the hall, near the foot of marble stairs that rose dimly toward the top floor, she stopped beside an open doorway. "And this is your room."

I stepped past her into a room that held a bed with a dark red velvet canopy, a wardrobe with elaborately carved doors of some dark wood, a dressing table skirted with red velvet, and a washstand bearing a basin and pitcher, both ornamented with painted vine leaves. Thankfully, I noticed that here the marble floor was covered with a worn but still lovely Persian carpet.

From the doorway Maria asked, "Is Emilio bringing the rest of your luggage?"

"Yes. He'll bring my trunk from the station tomorrow."

"Very well. I will tell the Contessa that you will be in to see her soon." She paused. "It is best not to disturb her after eleven o'clock. She is frail, although she does not like others to realize it."

There had been a note almost of tenderness in her voice. No matter how others might view my great-aunt, obviously her housekeeper felt affection as well as respect for her.

"I will hurry. Thank you, Maria."

She left, closing the door behind her. Quickly I took off my jacket and freshened up as best I could with lukewarm water from the pitcher. No time to unpack the valise Emilio had left at the foot of the bed. As I was smoothing my hair, I noticed that the velvet dressing table skirt, like the canopy of the bed, was worn almost through in spots. Well, that did not matter. The room appeared comfortable, if not exactly cheerful. And apparently there was a balcony beyond those long glass doors.

I took a few seconds to make sure. Yes, it was a balcony, projecting out over the side canal, whose dully gleaming black surface was no longer dimpled by raindrops. Looking down to my left, I could see the gondola and the little skiff, moving gently at their moorings. I glanced at the low-walled garden directly across the canal, and at the darkened house rising beyond it. As I turned back toward the glass doors, I noticed that there were other balconies projecting from this floor, one of them bathed in light from the room behind it. Then I went into my room, gave a last hasty look at my mirrored reflection, and moved out into the hall.

I had gone only a few steps when I stopped short, arrested by the sight of a small figure standing in a darkened doorway. For a dreadful moment I thought the figure had two heads, one that of child of about eight, the other much smaller, and disfigured with thick facial hair. Then I saw that the second head was that of a monkey peering over the little girl's shoulder.

The dark-haired child, snub-nosed and wide of mouth, could have been no beauty, even at her best. But when, after staring at me for a moment, she drew her mouth down at the corners with her two little fingers and rolled her eyes back until only the whites showed, she looked even less human than her furry companion.

For an absurd moment I felt a little frightened by the grimacing child and by the monkey, now hurling simian curses at me. Then my sense of proportion reasserted itself. She was only a little girl making a face.

I took a step backward, threw up both hands, and rolled my eyes in simulated terror.

The little girl took her fingers down from her mouth. The surprised, respectful look she gave me made me think that I was the first adult who, instead of showing indignation or distaste, had joined in her little game. Then she stepped backward and closed the door.

As I went on down the hall, I wondered who she was. Certainly not a servant's child, not on this floor. And not Isabella's. Carlo had said that his sister had no children. Then could the child be the offspring of the Contessa's other grandson? No, Carlo had told me that his younger brother was not married, nor—and this he conveyed with a shrug, a smile—was likely to be.

As I approached the Contessa's door, the prospect of the coming interview crowded the child from my thoughts. The next few minutes would determine whether I, who had lost so much in these past few months, could achieve usefulness and at least a measure of peace in this island city and this canal-girt house.

CHAPTER 2

I KNOCKED on the door.

The voice that bade me come in was old and harsh, more like that of a man, and yet surprisingly strong for someone of eighty-odd. As I entered the room, I had an impression of wall lamps in crystal brackets, of a frescoed ceiling where a semi-nude classic figure floated among clouds, of walls covered in frayed yellow damask, and of a fire flickering beyond an elaborately carved marble mantelpiece. Then all my attention centered on the woman who sat as if enthroned in a wheelchair, its back padded with red plush, close to the fire—Sophia Belzoni, widow of Count Antonio Belzoni, and daughter of the ancient Venetian house of Verracio.

It was like looking at an older, sterner version of the adored grandmother who had died when I was fifteen. Here again was the Verracio nose, delicately aristocratic in my grandmother's case, strong and more aquiline in her sister's. My grandmother's green eyes, even when she was in her mid-seventies, would twinkle at me with affectionate, almost girlish amusement. Great-aunt Sophia's faded green eyes looked at me shrewdly, and the rather wide Verracio mouth, so mobile in my memories of my grandmother, was curved by only the faintest of smiles.

"Come closer," the harsh voice said. "Let me look at you."

Nerves taut, I crossed the room and stood before her. She was wearing, I noticed now, a green velvet robe with a collar of worn brown fur. What should I call her? Contessa? Madame? Aunt Sophia?

"You're very thin."

"Yes," I said, wondering when she would ask me to sit down. "I've lost quite a lot of weight recently."

Her voice held a kind of sardonic sympathy. "I suppose you've had reason." She paused. "You speak excellent Italian."

"My grandmother taught me from the time I was a small child."

"She's the one I want to hear about. Sit down."

I took the only nearby seat, a tall armchair, its back padded with red velvet, which stood on the opposite side of the fireplace. It must have been designed during the last century, when, my grandmother had told me, cabinetmakers had indulged to the full that Venetian taste for the grotesque. Spiny-backed dragons writhed along its arms, so that it would have been impossible to rest your hands upon them.

She leaned forward. "Tell me, was my sister happy, living over there among savages?"

I felt startled, and then resentful. Waiting until I was sure I would sound calm, I said, "If you mean Indians, there have been no hostile Indians in Connecticut since before the Revolution."

She ignored that. "I don't see how she could have been happy." There was avidity in her face. I caught a glimpse of an ancient rivalry, surviving into the Contessa's old age, surviving even the death of her sister.

Although I knew it was not the answer she wanted, I said, "I think she was very happy."

"Even after her husband lost his money?" Her voice was incredulous. "The money was the only reason my father consented to the marriage, you know."

I did know. My grandmother had told me that ever since the late seventeenth century, when Venice's once-flourishing world trade had begun to decline, the Verracios and other Venetian nobility had lived in increasing poverty behind the moldering façades of their great houses.

But my grandfather had possessed money. Owner of a shipping line while still a young man, he had come to Venice in the eighteen-twenties to negotiate a trading agreement with manufacturers of Venetian glass. There he had married a vivacious beauty named Angela Verracio, brought her to New York, and installed her in a Fifth Avenue mansion.

Five years later the mansion and most of his fortune were gone, drained away by the loss at sea of two of his ships, and by his ill-fated efforts to recoup his losses by investing in a railroad line. As the owner of ships trading with Cuba, he had gained some knowledge of tobacco culture, and so he used what money he had left to buy a Connecticut tobacco farm. There his only offspring, my father, was born. There as a child and young girl, I used to visit my widowed grandmother, sitting with her in the sunny kitchen while we chatted in the liquid Venetian Italian she had taught me.

"Of course," the Contessa said, "I was glad to see her married, even to an American. She had refused most of the young men in Venice. And until she was married, my father was reluctant to allow me to marry Antonio Belzoni. In our family it was a tradition that the elder daughter be married first."

I must have looked startled, because she said, "Oh, yes. Angela was a year older than I. If she were alive now, she would be eighty-four."

"Yes, I suppose so." When would she turn from this talk of herself and her sister and ask if I were tired from my long journey, and how I liked my room? When would she comment on my letter to her, outlining my situation, and asking for shelter and employment?

She said, "I suppose the real reason you wanted to come to Venice is that you're in love with my grandson."

I said, astonished, "With Carlo?"

I thought of the one time I had met my Venetian second

cousin, that ill-fated day I had journeyed to New York to hear him sing the leading male role in a matinee performance of *La Traviata*. Afterwards he had stood there in his dressing room, still in make-up and costume, his handsome face reflecting his pleasure in the applause he had received, and in the adoring attention of the fashionable women surrounding him. His manner to me, an American cousin of whose existence he must have been scarcely aware, had been not only flatteringly gallant; it had seemed to hold even a little genuine warmth.

I had liked him well enough. And later on I had been grateful for his half-jocular suggestion that I become his grandmother's paid companion. But in love with him? How could one even know what he was really like—a man who could enact the role of an Egyptian king one day, a medieval knight the next, and a modern young Frenchman the next—let alone fall in love with him? No, even if I could free myself from my helpless longing for Caleb Hayworth, I would not feel attracted to my cousin.

"No, I am not in love with Carlo."

The shrewd old eyes studied my face. "Yes, I can see that you're not—which is strange, because even women old enough to know better fall in love with him." She paused. "Are you in love with someone else?"

Resenting the pain her question brought me, I said, "No."

"Why not? I know you Anglo-Saxon women are cold, but still, I should think that by the time you're twenty-three— Didn't you say in your letter that you were twenty-three?"

Cold! I thought of Caleb striding through the Connecticut moonlight across the lawn of my father's house. I thought of myself, unable to wait for the feel of his arms around me, running to meet him. "I'll be twenty-four in July," I said.

"And you haven't wanted to marry?"

"I was engaged. It was broken off some months ago, around the time of my father's death."

"Why was it broken off?"

That I was not going to tell her. "We decided that we were not suited to each other."

She looked annoyed for a moment, and then gave a slight smile, as if acknowledging defeat. "Your letter did not mention your mother. Is she dead?"

"She died when I was five."

"And your father. What did he die of?"

"A stroke, a second one."

That was what the doctor had written on the death certificate. But I knew that the true cause was the knowledge that he, after a long and honorable career as a history professor in the small college near our town, was about to be revealed as the perpetrator of a fraud. True, his sole motive had been to provide me with a legacy. But nonetheless his act was as fraudulent as if he had sold a fake diamond as a real one.

"I suppose it was after his death that you became a companion to the elderly woman you wrote me about."

"Housekeeper-companion."

The position had been a godsend. My father, just as he had feared would be the case, had left me almost nothing. Even our house, near the college where he had taught until his retirement, was heavily mortgaged. By letter I applied for teaching posts in several girls' schools. Since the fall term was well under way, I had little hope of favorable replies, and received none. Then an old friend of my father's, a semi-invalid named Mrs. Wentworth, sent me a note by her maid, Anastasia. Her former housekeeper had retired. Would I accept the post, just until I secured a teaching position?

Later, in her bedroom in the big white house her husband had left her, she explained to me that my duties would be light. Although semi-paralyzed, she was able to get about with a cane, and so would need little in the way of nursing. Mainly I would supervise Anastasia, who was loyal and hard-working, but far from bright. After fourteen years in Mrs. Wentworth's service, she could not keep household accounts or plan even the simplest menus.

"You didn't mind being a servant?" A hint of cruelty in the old voice made me think she wanted me to wonder about my status in her own eyes. Would she consider me primarily as a grandniece or a servant?

"No, I didn't mind." In fact, I had enjoyed my duties and my daily conversations with Mrs. Wentworth, who, despite her crippled state, was a woman of lively and varied interests.

"The fire in her house. Why weren't you there at the time?"

"I had gone to New York to the Metropolitan Opera House."

"To hear Carlo?"

"Yes."

I went on to explain that it was in a copy of Mrs. Wentworth's *Harper's Magazine* that I had read an advertisement for my famous cousin's coming appearance at the Metropolitan. Take the train to New York, Mrs. Wentworth had urged me, and go to a matinee. She would have Anastasia's assistance if she needed it.

I objected that her doctor had given strict orders that I, not Anastasia, was to measure out her medicine and see to it that her meals followed her prescribed diet. She had answered that she herself would measure out her medicine. As for her light supper, I could prepare a stew of lean meat and vegetables, and leave it in the ice chest for Anastasia to heat and serve.

In New York I had sat amid the gilt-and-red-plush splendor of the brand-new opera house, enthralled by Carlo Belzoni's golden tenor. Between the first and second acts I had sent a note backstage by an usher. The reply the usher brought me had a typically Italianate, or perhaps just theatrical, extravagance. "Come to my dressing room, dear unknown cousin, or I shall be desolated."

It was almost traintime when I left Carlo's crowded dressing room, with its clashing perfumes and babble of women's voices. I hurried through the early winter dusk toward Grand Central.

"Was the house still afire when you reached it?"

"Yes."

From the Three Rivers station platform I saw the reddish glow in the sky and knew, with a leap of terror, that it was the Wentworth house, or one nearby. The driver of the one-horse cab that met all trains apparently had gone to the fire. At least he was nowhere in sight. I picked up my skirts and ran down the cracked sidewalk beneath the leafless trees, urged on by my guilty fear despite an increasing pain in my side.

"How did the fire start?"

"They think an oil lamp turned over in the kitchen." A fireman, dragging a hose over the lawn toward the still blazing house, had told me that. "Probably the cat knocked it over. The flames and smoke must have awakened Mrs. Wentworth. Anyway, she—she'd tried to escape. But in the hall her cane had slipped, and she'd fallen. The flames didn't touch her. It was smoke that killed her."

I swallowed hard and then said, "They had taken her body away by the time I got there."

"And the maid. Wasn't she in the house?"

"No, she hadn't been there since right after she had served Mrs. Wentworth's supper."

I thought bitterly of Anastasia, that not-bright but loyal servant. What neither Mrs. Wentworth nor I knew—what no one knew until a frightened and sobbing Anastasia appeared to confess it the next day—was that she, at the age of thirty-four, had fallen in love with a nineteen-year-old boy, the son of a widowed laundress. Because he was too afraid of his mother to risk being seen at the Wentworth house, Anastasia had been stealing out at night to meet him in the woods north of town.

But no one blamed poor, stupid Anastasia. I was the one they blamed. I, to whom Mrs. Wentworth's doctor had given strict orders about her care. True, the coroner's verdict was accidental death, not "death through the criminal negligence of Sara Randall." But I could read that second verdict in the eyes of my fellow townsmen. I knew that some of them, too, must have remembered my poor, rash father and thought, "There must be something wrong in the Randall blood."

After the verdict I returned to my father's house, which was already in the process of being sold, and sat down at his desk and wrote to the Contessa Sophia Belzoni at the address her grandson had given me. I explained that I had almost no money, and that my equity in the house would bring me only about five hundred dollars. I wrote briefly about the fire and the resulting attitude of the townspeople. And then I told her how Carlo had said, "You're employed as a companion? Come to Venice and be a companion to my grandmother." I did not add that he had also said, "She's usually in need of a new one."

Several weeks after I mailed the letter, I received a cabled reply: "Come at once."

Now my great-aunt said, "I hope you will pay stricter attention to your duties in this household."

"Yes," I said, still wondering what to call her. "Just what are those duties?"

"I don't think you will find them onerous. At times, if Maria Rugazzi is otherwise occupied, I may want you to help me in or out of bed."

I nodded, wondering about the exact nature of her handicap.

She said, as if aware of my unasked question, "I am not paralyzed. It is only that rheumatism makes it hard for me to get about."

Again I nodded.

"And you will read to me. I imagine you read well. My last companion, this Scotswoman, read Italian well enough, but she was always getting head colds. That was why I had to dismiss her. Since then I've had no one but Maria to read to me, and she stumbles over every third word."

She added, "I hope you're not subject to head colds."

"I'm not." Which is fortunate, I thought, if I'm to live in this draughty marble pile.

"In return for this, you will receive food and lodging, and a salary." She named a sum, in liras, which amounted to only a small fraction of the generous twenty dollars a month Mrs. Wentworth had paid me. Well, I had no choice but to accept it. Even if I had wanted to return to Three Rivers, my remaining funds would not have paid my passage.

"Breakfast will be brought to your room," the Contessa continued. "From eleven in the morning on, you will find a cold buffet luncheon in the dining room. At night, of course, you will dine with Isabella and Giuseppe, and with Carlo, too, since he will probably arrive tomorrow."

Giuseppe? Oh, yes. Carlo had referred to his younger brother as Giuseppe.

"My tenant also sometimes takes dinner with my grandchildren, although I hear he prefers cafés such as the Quadri and the Florian."

"Your tenant!"

"Yes. He came here about two weeks ago and asked if we could provide lodging. He would much prefer to stay, he said, in a historic house such as this one rather than a hotel. He was obviously a gentleman, so I consented. Since many of the rooms on this floor are badly in need of replastering, I offered him the largest of the rooms on the fourth floor."

She added, in a self-congratulatory tone, "The money he is paying for the room more than covers the servants' wages."

That I could well believe, if the servants' wages were on the same scale as my salary. I asked, "Will I have other duties?"

"Yes, but I will tell you about them in the morning. I am tired now. Please help me to bed."

I wheeled her chair over to the bed, with its elaborately carved and gilded headboard upon which fat cupids embraced and doves flew with ivy sprigs in their beaks. I turned back the gold brocade spread. I helped her to stand and to remove the robe which covered her plain linen nightdress. She smelled of dry skin and sachet.

When she was in bed, I looked at the wall lamps burning in their crystal brackets and asked, "Shall I put out the lights?"

"No. Maria will be in shortly. She will do it."

"Well, good night, Contessa." I hesitated. "Is that what you would prefer me to call you?"

From the amusement in her eyes I realized that she had known all along I was wondering about that. "You are my sister's granddaughter. Naturally you will call me Aunt Sophia."

"Good night, Aunt Sophia."

I went out into the hall. Except at this end, the wall lamps had been extinguished, so that I could barely make out the staircase, rising to the fourth floor, at the other end. As I passed the room where the little girl had stood in the doorway, I realized that I still did not know who she was. Well, in the morning I would ask my great-aunt.

I was about to open the door of my room when I heard rapid footsteps, masculine ones, on the stairs leading down from the fourth floor. Some instinct told me that he must have been waiting up there. Inexplicably apprehensive, I turned, and then grew rigid with shock.

Caleb Hayworth stood on the landing, looking down at me.

CHAPTER 3

He came down the lower flight of stairs and moved toward me with that long, easy stride which always suggested the playing field rather than the classroom. He was smiling, but even in that dim light I could see the tension in his bony face.

"Hello, Sara."

I looked up at him, feeling pain and anger, and, to my shame, a longing to be held close to his tall body. My voice shook. "What are you doing here?"

"I live here, at the moment. I have paid two months' advance rent on what I suppose was once the major-domo's room. Anyway, it's the first one on the right as you enter the servants' quarters."

"Did you know I was coming here?"

"Of course. Otherwise I wouldn't be in Venice."

"How did you know?"

"Mrs. Gamp wrote to me in London. It was a long letter, telling about the fire and the inquest, and that you'd sailed for Italy to live with your Venetian relatives. I'd given the last of my lectures at the university, and so I was free to come here."

Mrs. Gamp was not a woman. His real name was Charles Bascomb, and he was a professor of English literature at the small Connecticut college where my father had once taught. Because of his love of gossip, particularly the malicious sort, Professor Bascomb's associates had nicknamed him after the Dickens character.

I said, "It was cruel of you to come here. It was loathsome."

"Sara, listen to me. You need me now. You can't exile yourself here in Venice."

"Need you! Need you to remind me of what you did?"

"I did what I had to do."

"You killed my father!"

"Sara, Sara! A stroke killed your father."

"It was you who caused it, threatening him, humiliating him."

His face had become somber. "You still don't understand the gravity of what he did, do you?"

I remained silent. The truth was, I did understand. But I had loved him deeply, my stooped, gentle father. To this moment I was tortured by the thought of what his last hours must have been as he cowered there in his locked study among the mementos of his long and honorable career—his framed diplomas, his citation from the New England Historical Society for his discovery of the Martha Washington correspondence, and his letter from President Grant praising his monograph on Zachary Taylor.

"Go away. Go back to Oxford, or wherever you've been."

"London. I've been lecturing at London University. And I won't go back." He smiled faintly. "Unless the ceiling of my room caves in, which is not unlikely, I'll stay here until my rent is up."

"Why?"

"Because I think you'll change your mind. Frankly, I'm counting on the Belzonis. I don't think you will stand living here with that greedy old pirate of a Contessa and her mincing grandson and her high-born wanton of a granddaughter, Signora Ponzi."

"I might have known. Since you had no sympathy for my father, I could scarcely expect you to like my Italian relatives."

"That's not fair. I had great sympathy for your father, and I liked him. You know I did."

There was no point in our going around and around, squirrel-like, in that same bitter argument. "Good night, Caleb." I went inside my room, closed the door, and stood with my hand on the knob. After a moment I heard his footsteps ascending the stairs. He would have to leave. I had crossed an ocean hoping to find, not just a livelihood, but a measure of peace. And now here was Caleb, reminding me of everything I had hoped to forget.

I unpacked my valise and hung my cloak and two dresses in the tall old wardrobe. I undressed and extinguished the oil lamp standing on the dressing table. Then, wearing a yellow flannel robe over my nightdress, I stepped out on the balcony. The air was warmer now, and a glance upward showed me that stars shone between rents in the scudding clouds.

After a moment I had a sense of the city stretching darkly around me in the maze of canals and narrow streets and steeply pitched footbridges my grandmother had described to me. How still Venice was late at night, even more so than my Connecticut village, because there, almost any night, you could hear the sough of wind through tall elms, and the occasional passage of someone on horseback or in a buggy along the street. But trees in watery Venice must be few. And my grandmother had told me that along the meandering streets no wheels turn, ever, not even those of a child's roller skate.

And then the wind must have changed, because once again I heard the distant thunder of storm-driven surf against the lagoon's barrier beach. I thought of Emilio's coarsely handsome face, watching me for some sign of horror as he predicted the Adriatic roaring into the lagoon.

While I looked down at the walled garden across the canal, other faces seemed to rise from its darkness to float before my weary eyes. Maria Rugazzi's strong peasant face in its frame of gray-threaded black hair. The lovely pictured face of my Cousin Isabella, and the face of her absent older brother, smiling through its heavy theatrical make-up. The face of Sophia Verracio Belzoni, with its faded but shrewd green eyes, and its nose like the prow of a ship. The grimacing face of that child with the chattering monkey. And Caleb's face . . .

He would have to leave. I would make him leave. But I would not think about that tonight. I was tired, tired, tired.

Turning, I went back into my room.

CHAPTER 4

A KNOCK on the door awoke me. I sat up in bed, aware of bright sunlight streaming in through the balcony windows, and asked, "Who is it?"

A puzzled feminine voice countered in Italian, "What did you say, signorina?"

I realized I had spoken in English. When I repeated my question in Italian, the woman answered, "It is Louisa, signorina. I have brought your breakfast."

The door opened, and a slender girl in a maid's uniform came in, wheeling a breakfast cart. She was about nineteen, I judged, and pretty, with a skin of northern Italian fairness and curly dark hair set off by a starched white cap.

"Thank you," I said, and got out of bed.

I had expected her to leave the room. Instead she retreated a few steps toward the door and then just stood there. As I put on my robe and splashed cold water from the basin onto my face and dried it with the washstand towel, I was aware of her dark eyes fixed unwinkingly upon me. I was to grow used to that Venetian gaze, a flat stare of sheer curiosity.

I said, turning toward her, "Is there something—?"

"I am waiting to pour your chocolate."

I sat down in the room's one chair, a fragile-looking armless chair covered in worn red plush. Louisa poured chocolate into a cup and lifted the lid of a silver dish to reveal sweet buns. Even after I had taken a sip of chocolate and a bite of the warm, flaky pastry, she still had not left. Well, if she was to stay here, we might as well talk.

"Does the Contessa keep a large staff?"

"Oh, no. There is Maria Rugazzi, and Emilio— You have seen Emilio?"

"Yes. He brought me from the station last night."

"He is conceited, that one. He thinks that because he can read a little, he is very smart, although he is really quite stupid. And he thinks all he has to do is to look at a girl. But then, it is to be expected. His father is from Naples."

Inwardly I smiled. My grandmother had told me that Venetians of all classes regard, not just foreigners, but the residents of other Italian cities with scorn, or at best amused tolerance.

"And there is the other housemaid, Hortensia. Hortensia does not like me, because I am young and pretty. And she does not like the Contessa, because fifteen years ago she was in love with the cook here, and the Contessa dismissed him, and he went to work for another family and married one of the maids there."

"Who is your cook now?"

"Giovanni. He is very fat and short-tempered, but he is the best cook in Venice."

That was pleasant news. But it was hard to believe that my penurious great-aunt would pay the wages of the best cook in Venice.

"Once Giovanni almost killed a man," Louisa said. "He went to prison for it. After he was released, no other family wanted him, and so the Contessa was able to hire him very cheaply."

"Oh, I see. Then there are five servants in all. That seems to me like a large staff."

"Oh, no, signorina. I have heard that for a time after this house was built, there were thirty servants living on the top floor, not just along the rear of the house where we live now, but in the empty rooms above this one, and in the empty top-floor rooms on the other side of the court."

She paused, and then added, "Now someone who is not a servant is living on the top floor. An English gentleman."

I said, before I thought, "He's an American."

"Signore Hayworth? But is he not from London?"

"He has been teaching at a school there. But he was born in Boston. That's an American city."

Others besides this little maid had been confused about Caleb Hayworth's nationality. The son of a State Department official, he had grown up in consulates in Rome, Paris, and London. After graduating from Oxford with a first in history, he had become a teaching fellow there.

It was this cosmopolitan background, as well as the papers he had published on seventeenth-century Anglo-American history, which had made my father's little college so proud to have him as a guest lecturer for last year's summer session. When my father told me he had invited Caleb Hayworth for dinner, I had expected to meet some rumpled, narrow-shouldered young man with his hair falling into his eyes. Then I had opened the front door and seen him standing there on the porch, a tall man with the muscular neck and shoulders of an oarsman, and dark blond hair gilded by the sunset. Even in that first moment, I had felt the strong pull of his physical attractiveness.

"He is handsome, that American." She sighed. "But very correct."

I could imagine her dark eyes, as she passed him in a hall, looking up with demure invitation. But his response had been "correct." And why, I asked myself angrily, should I feel pleased by that? Why should I still care whether or not Caleb responded to other women?

My annoyance with myself sharpened my voice. "I don't want to keep you from your work, Louisa."

"Yes, I suppose I must leave." She started to turn away. "Oh,

I almost forgot. The Contessa wants you to come to her room after breakfast."

"Very well, as soon as I am dressed."

Out in the hall a few minutes later, I paused beside one of the long windows that lined the left wall. Yes, these windows overlooked the grand salon's copper-sheathed roof, greenish in the sunlight, and faced two floors of windows across the court. I wondered briefly if the rooms of the Contessa's grandchildren were over there or on this side of the house. Then I moved on down the hall.

When I entered my great-aunt's room, I found her still in bed. Light spilling through the long windows, which I realized must overlook the Grand Canal, showed me that the big room was even shabbier than it had seemed the night before, with actual rents in the damask-covered walls, and threadbare spots in the Aubusson carpet. But it also showed me, when I stole a glance upward, that the goddess floating against the blue, cloud-dotted ceiling probably had been painted by Tiepolo.

This morning, the Contessa told me, she would not get up for a while. Then she added, "Why did you put on that same dress?"

"My trunk has not arrived from the station."

"In Venice only lower-class women or those in mourning wear dark colors. I know it is different with you Anglo-Saxons. It is the influence of your frumpy queen, no doubt."

I forbore pointing out that Victoria was not "my" queen. Obviously she thought, or pretended to think, that America was still a raw frontier, where homespun-clad subjects of the British Crown were besieged by Indians.

"Sit down," she said.

When I had drawn a straight chair up beside her bed, she went on, "You asked about your other duties. Your chief duty will be to instruct Anna. In fact, Anna is the real reason I wanted you to come here. You can follow the curriculum the Scotswoman drew up as suitable for an eight-year-old."

So that was the name of the little girl with the pet monkey. I ventured, "Who is she?"

"My great-grandchild." Her voice became bitter. "Almost certainly the only great-grandchild I will ever have."

"Is she Isabella's child?"

"She is not! In six years Isabella and that husband of hers have produced no children. And Giuseppe is interested only in furniture and window draperies and such frippery. My one hope of a male great-grandchild rests with Carlo."

She drew a deep, angry breath and then went on, "When he arrives, I again will try to persuade him that his duty to all of us is to marry." She added, with warning significance, "To marry a rich woman."

So, despite my protestations, she still suspected that I had come to Venice to set my cap for Carlo.

"I doubt that I will succeed," she went on. "Carlo prefers to travel about the world, performing on stage like some cheap mountebank, and pursuing married women."

How different was his grandmother's view from that of the rest of the world. To others the great operatic tenor, Carlo Belzoni, was an enviable figure. But in the eyes of this old aristocrat, his behavior was undignified, and perhaps even traitorous to his family and his class.

I said, "I don't understand about Anna. Whose child is she?"

"My eldest grandson's, the only one of my grandchildren who pleased me. He was a soldier, my Antonio, a captain of infantry. And he died," she said, staring straight ahead. "He died of lung fever, like his mother and father before him. Venice has always been a bad place for those with weak chests. The dampness . . ."

Her voice trailed off. After a moment I asked, "Is the child's mother also dead?"

Her gaze swung to me. "I have no idea," she said coldly. Then, as I looked at her in confusion, she went on, "The child's mother was Rosa Rugazzi, the daughter of my housekeeper, Maria Rugazzi. Rosa was also a servant here."

I said incredulously, "You mean your favorite grandson married—"

"Of course he did not marry her! She came to me and told me that she was to have a child, and that Antonio was the father. I was inclined to believe her, because he was attractive to women, my Antonio, and because she was the one who served his breakfast and took care of his room whenever he was here. But of course I would not take her unsupported word for it. I wrote to Antonio. He was so ill by then that I had sent him to a sanitarium in the hills around Padua, hoping he would recover."

Again she stared broodingly ahead. "He was dying by then, and too weak to hold a pen. Not that his letter said so. Being Antonio, he wanted to spare me grief as long as possible. He said it was because he had injured his hand that he was dictating the letter to another patient. But anyway, he acknowledged that the child was his. Two weeks later his lung hemorrhaged, and he died."

She fell silent. After a moment I said, "And the child?"

"She was born five months later. I acknowledged her as my great-grandchild, and legally adopted her, so that she could bear the name Anna Belzoni."

"How did the mother—"

"She accepted the arrangement. I dismissed her from my service after giving her money." She named in liras a sum equivalent to about three hundred and fifty dollars.

"And you don't know where she is now?"

"I heard that she took the money to Rome, rented lodgings, and set herself up as a common courtesan. Whether she's still there or not, I have no idea."

I looked at her in stunned silence. She had dismissed Maria Rugazzi's daughter—quite literally onto the streets, as it had turned out. And yet Maria had stayed on here as housekeeper.

What was more, she unmistakably felt an affectionate respect for her employer. Perhaps both women, ruthlessly applying a double standard of sex and class, had regarded Rosa as hopelessly fallen. And perhaps both women, the aristocratic great-grandmother and the servant-class grandmother, regarded the child Anna as a strong link between them.

I felt suddenly very American and unsophisticated, and all at sea in this world with its ruthlessness, its rigid class consciousness, and its values so different from those of the democratic, hard-working, and puritanical New England in which I had grown up.

"Will you be able to teach the child? Your letter said that you had applied for teaching posts, so I imagine you have some qualifications."

"I have a certificate from a two-year normal school in Connecticut."

"Well, then?"

"It depends upon what you want taught. I have little knowledge of mathematics or the sciences."

She waved her thick-veined hand dismissingly. "What good would such subjects be to her? I would like her to continue with her Venetian history and her English. You might deepen and broaden her knowledge of art—that is, if you yourself have any such knowledge." She paused. "I saw you look up at the ceiling fresco when you came in. Who do you suppose was the artist?"

"Tiepolo?"

She nodded. "How did you know?"

"We have museums in America, and books of art reproductions. We even have a few artists of our own. You may have heard of Stuart, for instance, or Whistler."

"You're becoming impertinent," she said, but she sounded diverted rather than annoyed. "Tell me what you think of the other paintings in this room."

Rising, I began to wander along the rows of paintings, most

of them small but in elaborately carved gilt frames which hung on the damask walls. Scenes of masked balls and card parties and carnivals by Longhi, landscapes by Guardi, religious subjects by Carriera. In this one room hung a respectable fortune in Venetian art. And yet in other rooms all over this enormous house, probably, plaster was cracking, and ceilings threatening to fall, and fabrics fraying. It was evident that people like the Verracios and Belzonis, unless very hard-pressed indeed, did not sell their family treasures. Instead they sought to acquire money in other ways, such as marrying it.

I turned back to the Contessa. "I like these pictures."

"I could tell you did. Come here." As I moved toward her, she pointed at a framed parchment hanging beside the gilded headboard. "Did you notice this? It was done three hundred years ago, at the order of an ancestor of mine. It is not worth as much as any of the paintings, but I value it highly."

It was a map of the lagoon showing Venice and its sister islands—fairly large islands such as Murano and Torcello, and tiny ones like Santo Spirito—each labeled in minuscule red script. Three hundred years ago, I thought. The sixteenth century. Then the Republic of Venice was still the richest and most powerful of the Italian city-states, the waters of its lagoon plowed by galleons coming in on the tide to bring silks and jewels from the orient, spices from India, and precious woods from Madagascar to the proudest, most luxury-loving, and most profligate city in Europe.

For the first time I fully realized that ancestors of mine were in Venice then. They must have watched the galleons come in on the tide. And later those who could afford to had strolled in new finery through the Piazza San Marco, that great square I had not as yet seen, among the swaggering ship's officers, and the jugglers, and the noble ladies in those ridiculous *chopines* I had read about—shoes with soles a foot and a half thick, so that they tottered about with their elaborate coiffures towering high above the crowd, and their hands resting for balance on the heads of the servants who had accompanied them. Yes, ancestors of mine had seen all that.

I felt a stir of excitement, as if the thought of those tide-borne galleons had set in motion some ancient tide in my own blood.

I looked down to meet the Contessa's gaze. It was so sharp that I felt she had sensed my reaction to the parchment map. She asked, "Do you want to see the most precious object in this house?"

"Of course, if you want to show it to me."

"Go out."

"I'm afraid I don't—"

"Leave the room. Close the door and wait until I call you."

Wondering, I obeyed. Through the closed door I could hear the creak of springs as she left the bed, then the faint sound of her movements about the room, and then again the creak of springs. "Come in."

When I entered, I saw that she was sitting up in bed with something on her lap, a basin of some dull yellow metal, its outer surface studded with colored stones. I asked, "Is it gold?"

"Yes, and the stones are real. There are topazes, rubies, opals, and one emerald."

"It must be very valuable indeed."

She nodded. "And not just because of its materials. It is very old. A Verracio brought it back from the sack of Constantinople more than six hundred years ago, and even then it was many centuries old." She paused. "There was a legend in Constantinople that this is the basin in which Pontius Pilate washed his hands after the judgment of Christ."

Aware of her narrowed gaze upon my face, I said nothing.

"Well, do you believe that?"

Not knowing what reply would be tactful, I gave her a truthful one. "I don't think the procurator of an obscure Roman province like Judea would have possessed such a rich object."

"I agree. But undoubtedly it predates the birth of Christ. Probably it was made for some ancient barbarian king in Asia Minor.

"Anna loves it," she added. "Often when she comes to this room I allow her to hold it."

I thought of the plain eight-year-old holding on her lap a priceless object that had survived two thousand years of bloody wars, and the ravishment of burning cities, and the rise and fall of empires.

The Contessa said, "You will give Anna her lessons from three to five in the afternoons. In the morning Maria teaches her to embroider and crochet."

Not, her grandmother teaches her. Maria. Did the child even know the housekeeper was her grandmother? Perhaps not. But I felt sure that in the privacy of this room the aged aristocrat and the aging servant exchanged worries and hopes about the child in whose veins their blood mingled.

"You may go now. I told Maria to bring Anna to your room for a few minutes at ten o'clock, so that you two can become acquainted."

"Shall I come back to you later?"

"Not unless I send for you."

I felt dismay. Was I expected to stay in my room, waiting for her possible summons? "I had hoped to see a little of Venice today."

"Do that. I won't need you until late afternoon, if then. If Emilio isn't busy, he can take you wherever you want to go."

"Thank you. I wish you a good morning, Aunt Sophia."

"Good morning, Sara."

As I moved down the hall, I thought of how unwise the Contessa was, for all her seeming shrewdness, not to have the Constantinople basin placed in a bank vault. To what hiding place, I wondered, was she restoring it right now? Was there a safe behind one of those paintings? Or did she, like many women, place more faith in unorthodox hiding places? I pictured her moving painfully across the room to place the basin in the disemboweled back of an ancient sofa.

CHAPTER 5

WHEN I ENTERED my room, I saw that my trunk still had not been delivered. I went to the wardrobe and looked disconsolately at the two dresses hanging there. One was a dinner gown of pale yellow silk—my only dinner gown—and the other a morning dress of printed muslin, a garment far too humble, I realized now, to be worn anywhere except in my own room. If I was to venture out this morning, and I was determined to, it would be in my brown traveling costume.

Someone knocked. "Come in," I said.

Maria Rugazzi entered, holding Anna by the hand. "Good morning, signorina. I have brought Anna Belzoni to meet you. Anna, this is Signorina Randall, who will give you your lessons."

The child curtsied, never taking her eyes from my face. They held the measuring look which, I imagine, must be in a pugilist's eyes as he confronts his opponent before the start of a match.

"The schoolroom adjoins Anna's bedroom, signorina. Paco is not to be allowed in there." Paco, I gathered, was the monkey. "Anna has agreed to that, haven't you, Anna?"

The child said in a resigned voice, "Yes, Maria." Whether or not the child knew that the woman beside her was her grandmother, she obviously respected her.

"Then I will leave you and the signorina together." She touched the child's dark hair briefly and turned to the door.

When the woman had gone, Anna bent her right leg at the knee and clasped her instep. "I'm not to be pushed at my lessons." She gave a hop. "I'm delicate."

I studied her. Her dark hair, loosely curling, might be a testament to her Belzoni blood. It reminded me of Carlo Belzoni's. The grayish-green eyes and the wide mouth might be an inheritance from the Verracios. But the pug nose must have been handed down to her by her mother. "You don't look delicate. However, I hope you'll like your lessons so much that you won't have to be pushed."

She said nothing, just dropped her clasped instep and put her foot on the floor, but her gaze held cynical disbelief.

"I'll come to your room at three," I said.

"Do you remember which room it is?"

"I remember. You frightened me. For a moment I thought you had two heads."

She looked so delighted that I thought she might make that hideous face again. Instead she said, "I must go to my grandmother now."

Thinking she might have used the wrong term, I asked, "Do you mean the Contessa?"

"No, the Contessa is my great-grandmother. Maria is my grandmother."

So she knew that. For Maria's sake, I was glad.

When she had gone, I tidied my hair, looked ruefully down at my brown bombazine dress, and then picked up my reticule. I left my room, went down the stairs past Isabella's portrait, and along the hall below. Now I noticed things that had escaped my attention the night before—the leaded panes of the tall windows set in the outside wall, and two life-sized ebony Moors, naked except for draped loincloths, who flanked the entrance to the grand salon, glaring fiercely from beneath peaked helmets. I descended the broad steps past the peeling mural of nymphs and satyrs, went through the opened wrought-iron doors, and crossed the grassy courtyard toward the landing stage. I could hear a young woman's voice now. "Do come with me!" she was saying. "You'll find it so amusing."

Isabella, I thought. Then, as I emerged from the archway, I saw, too late, that she was not alone. Caleb stood beside her, dark blond hair glinting in the sunlight. And farther along the landing, Emilio waited beside his graceful black craft.

My cousin's green eyes widened when she saw me. She was so lovely, almost as lovely as her portrait, in her flounced green dress of sheer lawn and her lacy white shawl, that I was conscious more than ever of my own sober and travel-worn attire.

"You must be Sara," she cried. Moving on slender green slippers to where I stood, she embraced me, touched her lips to my cheek, and then stood back to look at me. "How wonderful of you to have come all the way from America to be with us!"

The words were cordial enough, but a certain irony in her tone told me that she knew it was not a longing to be with my Venetian relatives that had sent me across the ocean. Probably everyone in the Belzoni house, including the servants, knew that I had fled my native town because I was almost without funds, and unable to bear the disapproval in the eyes of people I had known all my life. Well, if they knew, there was no help for it.

"Please forgive my appearance," I said. "My trunk hasn't yet come from the station."

"I am about to fetch it, signorina." Here, in the presence of the Contessa's granddaughter and of the tall American, Emilio's manner was no longer subtly insolent.

"And on the way to the station, he will leave me at the Teatro La Fenice. Some puppeteers from Paris are performing in the square there. I was trying to persuade Signore Hayworth to go. Perhaps you will come with us."

She broke off, and then said, "Oh, please forgive me. This is Signore Hayworth."

"We have met," Caleb said.

Her smile wavered. "Here? Or in America?"

"Both," Caleb said. "I was about to tell you why I can't go to see the puppets. I have arranged to show your cousin St. Mark's this morning."

Incredulity crossed her face. Then she smiled. "Of course. I can see why two fellow Americans would want to renew their acquaintance." Plainly she could think of no other reason why Caleb should prefer my company to her own bright presence. "Emilio can take you there as soon as he returns."

"Thank you," Caleb said, "but we will hire a public gondolier." He moved toward me. "Shall we go now?"

The effrontery of him! But what could I do? Make a scene before my cousin? "I'm ready."

He turned to Isabella. "Good-by. I'm sorry I can't see the puppets."

"We'll go tomorrow." She smiled at me. "Have a good time, Sara."

Hand lightly touching my elbow, he led me back through the wrought-iron doors and along a wide, echoing ground floor hall, empty except for three mammoth Chinese urns set on ebony stands, toward a pair of tall carved doors. On this warm morning they stood open, so that the marble ceiling beneath which we moved seemed alive with dancing reflections from the Grand Canal.

We descended marble steps and turned to our left along a narrow brick walk which ended abruptly in a public landing stage. I stood by, feeling a helpless resentment, while Caleb spoke briefly to a grizzled but powerful-looking gondolier.

I had hoped to enjoy it, my first daylight ride on the Grand Canal. But I had only a blurred impression of the traffic—barges and gondolas and rowed skiffs—and of the white and pink and faded red façades of the great old houses standing above their shimmering reflections. Not only Caleb's presence, but the summerlike heat was reminding me of last summer—

Connecticut fields starred with daisies, Connecticut nights heavy with the scent of honeysuckle, and in my heart a burgeoning joy.

It was in August that Caleb proposed that we marry, and received my immodestly eager assent. As we stood embraced on the darkened porch of my father's house, Caleb said, "I'll go in and speak to him."

"No. Let's don't tell him yet."

"Why not? Your father likes me."

"He likes you very much. But he will also be very sorry to lose me. I'd rather wait until he has fully recovered." The previous winter he had suffered a slight stroke, which had left him with a dragging right foot. "Dr. Wales says it will be only a few more weeks."

"All right." Smiling, he released me. "We have lots of time."

Yes, lots of time. I saw time stretching before us, golden with promise. I said, "He'd recover more quickly, the doctor tells me, if he didn't work so hard." As I spoke, I was aware of light from my father's upstairs study falling on the lawn.

"What is he working on? Another book?" Since his retirement my father had added two more volumes to his published works, one a history of the Plymouth Colony, the other a monograph on the two letters of Martha Washington which he had discovered in an old chest. Originally the chest had belonged to my great-grandfather, father of that Josiah Randall who had gone to Venice to negotiate a contract and had returned with a Venetian bride.

"No, he seems to be working on correspondence."

Always a great letter writer, my father since his retirement had expanded his correspondence to include historians, both professional and amateur, all over the world. Of late, too, several men—New York and Boston business and professional men to whom history was a hobby—had appeared at our door to climb the steps to my father's study.

"Come here," Caleb said. He drew me to him, and we talked no more about my father that evening.

In less than two weeks, I learned why that study lamp had been burning so late.

When my father came in to dinner that late August night, his thin face was pale with excitement, and his gray eyes were bright behind their glasses. He laid an envelope beside his plate. After we were both seated, I asked, "What do you have there?"

"Your future." Grinning like a boy, he handed me the envelope.

Inside was a check for twenty thousand dollars, made out to my father, and a letter. Like the check, it had been signed by Clarence Dillman, a well-known New York merchant. "I have decided to meet your asking price for the Governor Bradford document now in my possession," the letter said. "Like you, I feel the first announcement of its discovery should be made at the annual meeting of the Historical Society in Washington next month. It will be a proud moment for both of us."

I said dazedly, "Where—"

"In that same chest. The document had been hidden beneath the leather lining the bottom. It's coming to pieces now. That's how I saw the letter. It was written by the Governor of the Plymouth Colony, and apparently never sent. In it he states that he and several other Colonial leaders plan to seek eventual independence from the Crown. Imagine, Sara! More than a hundred years before the Declaration of Independence, there was revolutionary ferment in America."

I said, awed, "And it's lain hidden all these years."

"Naturally it was hidden. It was treasonable. It could have cost him and his friends their heads. I've been negotiating in strict secrecy with several men for weeks. And now this check."

He beamed at me. "I'll wager you thought your old father was going to leave you penniless."

I wanted to tell him that, in any event, my future would

have been provided for. But no. To tell him of Caleb right then would have been to dim his triumph.

I went around the table and kissed his cheek. "May I tell Caleb?"

"He's coming here tonight? All right, tell him. I'm sure he can keep a secret."

When I told Caleb that night, he looked momentarily stunned. Then he said slowly, "A document like that would shed a whole new light on the Pilgrims."

"Would? You mean does, don't you?"

After a moment he smiled. "Of course. Does. Listen, I have some news, too. I've been offered posts by two English universities. I'll have to write to them that I'm staying here."

"You'd better," I said.

Caleb was supposed to come to dinner the next night, but he did not. Dinner was long since over, and my father had gone up to his study, when Caleb finally appeared.

His face was white. "I went to New York today and persuaded Mr. Dillman to let me see the Bradford letter. It's a fake."

I stared at him, unable to speak.

"The parchment is genuine, although I don't know where your father got hold of it."

There had been a roll of unused parchment in the chest when my father found the Martha Washington letter.

"The ink appears authentically faded," he went on. "There are books on forged documents that describe the process for fading ink, but even so he did surprisingly well. Otherwise, though—well, his stroke must have affected his judgment, Sara. There are foolish anachronisms, such as a reference to Bradford's conversation with a man who had been dead for almost a year at the time their talk is supposed to have taken place."

I didn't protest his judgment. Caleb knew far too much about such matters for me to do that. I said with an effort, "Did you tell Mr. Dillman?"

"No. First I'm going upstairs to give your father a chance to admit his forgery and return the check."

"You are not going up there!"

"Sara, get out of my way. What do you want me to do? Say nothing?"

"Yes!"

"You can't mean that. Your father has tried to falsify his country's history, and for gain. That's worse than theft."

"Caleb, if you dare—"

Grasping my shoulders, he forced me aside and ran up the stairs. The study door opened and closed. Clinging to the newel post, I listened to their voices, quiet at first, then loud and angry, with my father's voice riding high and thin and old above Caleb's deep one.

When Caleb came swiftly down the stairs, the skin drawn tight across the strong planes of his face, I asked, "Did he—"

"He won't listen."

"What are you going to do?"

"Tell Dillman," he said, and strode toward the front door.

I went upstairs. The study door was locked, and my father would not open it. Everything would be all right, he told me through the panel. Caleb just had some crazy notion. "Go to bed, Sara."

After an almost sleepless night, I found the study door still locked. My father did not answer when I called to him. Terrified, I ran to a neighbor. He came back with me and broke down the study door. We found my father slumped over his desk. Later the doctor said that probably he had died before midnight.

The gondola was approaching wide steps now, edged with a forest of striped mooring poles. Caleb said, "Do you feel any differently from the way you did last night?"

"No."

"Do you remember what I told you that last day?"

That last day. The day before my father's funeral when, behind the drawn blinds of my father's house, I had told Caleb I could never marry him. Because of the dim light filtering through the yellowish shades, Caleb's wretched face had a wan hue, as if bathed in the last feeble glow of a dying sun. "I remember."

"I told you that in no time at all someone else would have discovered your father's forgery and confronted him with it."

"Perhaps. But you're the one who did."

His voice was flat. "Yes, I was the one who did. I had to. If I had it to do over, I'd still do it. Can't you understand that?"

"I can. Perhaps in time I would even be able to forgive it. But I could never forget it."

"All right, Sara. We won't talk about it, not for a while."

The gondola glided to a stop between two others moored before the wide steps. Caleb and I climbed to a scene familiar to me from Canaletto paintings, photographs, and the loving descriptions of my grandmother—the *piazzetta,* or little square, of St. Mark's, guarded by St. Theodore and the Lion of St. Mark atop their tall twin columns, and bordered on the right by the façade, all rosy stone lace and graceful colonnades, of the Doge's Palace. Ahead I could see the golden horses of Lysippus pawing the clear morning air from above the doorway of the many-domed church.

"Shall we go into St. Mark's?" Caleb asked. I nodded.

That morning, looking at the ancient map of the lagoon, I had felt the pull of my Venetian heritage. Now amid the overwhelming splendor of St. Mark's, my New England ancestry asserted itself. As Caleb and I, in the wake of tweed-clad English tourists, moved about the vast interior, I looked through the eyes of a long line of Presbyterian Randalls at elaborate mosaics, at murals glittering with gold leaf, at church vessels of gold and silver, studded with gems. It was all too rich, too gaudy, too *eastern.* Almost I expected to hear the chant of a muezzin calling the faithful to praise, not the Christian God, but Allah.

We emerged from the church to sit at one of the numerous

tables standing along one side of the enormous square. A waiter brought us small cups of coffee. Near us on a platform, musicians were tuning their instruments.

Caleb said, "I got the impression you don't like St. Mark's."

"It's very beautiful. But it seems to me it must have been built primarily for display, not worship."

"Exactly. If you want dim religious atmosphere, go to other Venetian churches. St. Mark's was meant to impress foreign visitors with the wealth and power of the Republic."

"Including looted wealth. Those beautiful horses up there, looted from Constantinople. And that statue of St. Theodore in the *piazzetta*. It's really a pagan Greek statue. Why," I said, warming to the subject, "they even stole the body of St. Mark! They broke into his tomb and smuggled him out of Alexandria under a load of cantaloupes."

"Sara, before you work yourself into a moral froth over the medieval Venetians, let me remind you of what we Americans have done—and only yesterday, from the prospective of history. We stole a whole continent from the Indians. How's that for grand theft?"

"That was different," I said, and I knew I would be at a loss if he asked me to explain how it was different.

Instead he said quietly, "Perhaps you just don't like Venice."

"I don't know." I looked at the vast square and its strollers. Some appeared to be English or German tourists, the men in knickerbockers, the women in bulky tweed jackets and matching skirts, cut short at the ankles. As for the rest, I judged from the insouciant smartness of their dress that they were Venetians. I looked at the campanile across the square, soaring thick and red through the crystal light, and at a cloud of pigeons, swirling up from the pavement to obscure the golden bubble domes of St. Mark's. I knew that the square had been here for many centuries. And yet it seemed to me unreal, as if it were a gigantic stage set, and the people who strolled upon it, actors.

"Venice is beautiful," I said, "but there is so much of the

fantastic mixed in with it." I thought of the carved dragons writhing along the arms of a chair in the Belzoni house, and the naked ebony Moors glaring from beneath their helmets. And I thought of a stone head affixed to a house front, which I had glimpsed just before the gondola left us at the *piazzetta* steps, a truly terrible head, tongue lolling from its mouth, lips leering as if at some scabrous jest. "There's something even sinister about Venice. For a stranger, it's like being at a carnival, where for all you know there may be a real death's-head behind that death's-head mask."

His voice was quiet. "For a stranger in your mood. Last summer you would have loved the beauty of Venice. And that bizarre quality you mention, that would only have enhanced the beauty."

Last summer, when we were lovers.

"Whatever does or does not happen between us," he said, "I hope you're not going to turn into one of those neurasthenic, life-denying women, looking down your nose at all you can't enjoy."

The conductor on the bandstand raised his baton. The opening strains of "O Sole Mio" soared over the Piazza, lush, banal, and yet so charged with passionate longing that I felt tears pressing behind my eyes.

"Why don't you go back to London?"

"No."

"There's no use in your staying here."

"Aren't you being a bit self-centered? True, you're what brought me to Venice. But the city has other attractions."

The churches and museums? The Teatro La Fenice? Or Isabella Belzoni Ponzi, whose husband was so frequently absent? A high-born wanton, he had called her last night. But to a rejected man, a beautiful wanton might prove attractive indeed. Well, what did that matter to me, who always in her mind's eye would see a gentle old man slumped across a desk?

"Let's go across to Florian's," he said, "and have lunch."

"No, thank you. I'd like to go back to the house for lunch."

He said, after a moment's silence, "From your tone I take it that you want to go back alone."

"Yes, please."

He signaled the waiter. "All right. We'll go to the landing, and I'll put you in a gondola."

CHAPTER 6

About twenty minutes later, I climbed the steps leading up from the ground floor of the Belzoni house and moved along the wide hall. As I started past the archway of the grand salon, I looked inside and met the dark gaze of a slender man in his late twenties. "Hello!" he said in Italian. I stopped, and he moved toward me. In dark trousers and a bottle-green velvet jacket, and with a brocade waistcoat buttoned over his frilled white shirt, he was as gorgeously arrayed as any of the dandies in the Piazza. "You," he said, "must be my cousin Sara."

His smile was so friendly, and he was so obviously eager to be liked, that instantly I warmed to him. "And you're Giuseppe."

"That's right. Will you advise me, Sara? I'm so worried."

Wondering, I moved with him across the salon. Against the far wall stood several straight chairs that had not been there when I glanced into the salon earlier that morning. Their backs were gilded, and their seats covered with worn petit point.

"Will they do?" he asked anxiously.

"For what?"

"For the masquerade ball. We're giving one, you know. Will they do? That petit point is so shabby."

"That won't show much at night. And after the room fills up—"

"I suppose you're right. I do wish there was money for new

fabric, though, but Grandmother says there isn't." He paused. "What do you think of my grandmother?"

I said after a moment, "She's quite remarkable."

His face brightened. "She is, isn't she? Does she speak English with you?"

"She hasn't so far."

"She speaks far better English than any of the rest of us. And she has such a truly superb manner. I'm the only one here who appreciates her. Isabella thinks of no one but herself, and Carlo is away most of the year. I wish," he added wistfully, "that Grandmother approved of me more."

"Oh, Giuseppe. I'm sure that she—"

"No, she doesn't approve of me. She thinks I should have interests besides this house. But why shouldn't I devote myself to this house? Ca' Belzoni was once one of the greatest houses on the Grand Canal. And it is still filled with beautiful things. But it's in such dreadful need of repair."

I said tentatively, "Perhaps if you sold a few paintings—"

"Never. Grandmother and I feel the same way about that. It's all too depressing. Let's not talk about it. Shall we have luncheon? I was afraid I would have to have it alone."

We went through another archway into a smaller room, set with graceful card tables and fragile-looking chairs, probably French. Dust lay so thick on the tables that you could scarcely see the flower garlands painted on the pale wood. In the room beyond that, a massive old sideboard stood beside a green baize door. On the sideboard someone had set out a platter of cold meats, a silver filigree basket of bread, and a bowl filled with green salad. We filled our plates and drew our chairs companionably close at the long table.

I enjoyed that luncheon. It was pleasant, after that bruising conversation in the Piazza, to listen to Giuseppe rattle on about furniture and draperies and clothes.

At one point he said tactfully, "I like your dress, Sara. I really do. But I hope you have lighter things. If you think today is warm, just wait. This may be one of those years when summer comes practically overnight."

"I have other clothes in my trunk. I imagine Emilio has brought it from the station by now."

"You've seen Emilio? Oh, of course. He must have brought you here. He's a remarkable person, quite above his station. He can read, you know."

A few minutes later I said, "Well, I'd better see if my trunk has come."

"I hope it has. Good-by, Sara. I'll see you at dinner. It's served in here, at eight, in case no one has told you."

My trunk was in my room. I unlocked it with the key from my reticule, placed its tray laden with gloves, a box of hair-pins, and other small articles on the bed, and began to hang clothing in the wardrobe.

An odd, scrambling noise out in the hall. I looked at the door and saw its knob turn. "Who's there?" I called. Receiving no answer, I crossed the room and opened the door.

A furry shape darted past me, leaped chattering onto the washstand, and squatted there, teeth bared in what might have been either a grin or a snarl. I looked at the monkey with alarm touched by repugnance. If I tried to seize his red leather collar, would he bite me?

"Paco! Go away!"

Instead he leaped to the bed and seized a folded ivory fan from the trunk's tray. My Venetian grandmother had given me that fan, a family heirloom, on my fourteenth birthday. With a cry, I started toward him. He leaped to the floor and, dodging my grab at his collar, ran out the door.

Moving after him into the hall, I saw him climbing the first flight of stairs with that rolling but swift monkey gait, my fan still clutched in his fist. I ran after him up to the landing, up a second flight of stairs, and through a narrow archway.

Abruptly I was in another world from the faded but splendid one below. Here the hall, so narrow that it scarcely would allow two people to pass each other, stretched between rows of closed doors. Through the dim light I could see Paco lumbering toward a flight of narrow stairs. As I pursued him, I saw with dismay that the door at the top of the stairs stood slightly ajar. He scrambled up the stairs and through the opening. As I climbed after him, I looked down to my right and saw more stairs, almost as narrow, descending to the regions below. Then I moved through the doorway and found myself in a vast attic.

Dim light from a row of begrimed circular windows along the rear wall showed me a wilderness of objects—broken statuary, a mammoth framed mirror with a crack across its face, a sedan chair, like an upended coffin, in which Belzoni ladies must once have been carried through the narrow streets. And everywhere there were boxes, barrels, and chests. The floor was so heavily coated with dust that I judged no one had been up here for months, perhaps years.

I could hear the monkey scrambling ahead of me through the maze. Following the sound, I squeezed between two stacks of heavy picture frames and went around an enormous wardrobe with a missing door. Now the scrambling sounds were to my right. I moved in pursuit and realized a moment later, still following the sound, that he was circling toward the attic door.

He let me catch up with him finally. I came around a group of upended carpet rolls, and there he was, perched on the back of a carved armchair with only one arm. I halted. "Paco! Give me that!"

Perhaps he was tired of the game. After chattering for a few seconds, he flung the fan away and leaped to a shelf that ran along the wall above the row of circular windows.

Bending, I retrieved my fan—and then stepped backward to avoid the cascade of objects dislodged by his lumbering progress along the shelf. Vases and small statuary, no doubt already cracked, shattered to bits on the floor. A small leather chest, its lid flying open, strewed envelopes at my feet. A bronze vase landed with the clangor of a gong. When he reached the end of the shelf, Paco leaped down and disappeared through the doorway.

Dismayed, belatedly aware that I'd had no right to invade this part of the house, I looked at the havoc my pursuit of the monkey had wrought among perhaps still-valuable objects. Sure that soon someone would climb the stairs to survey the litter and my disheveled appearance, I thrust the fan down the bosom of my dress and began to tidy up as best I could, picking up pieces of glazed vases and clay statuary and dropping them into a cracked terra cotta urn which stood on the floor against the wall. Yes, someone was coming now. I could hear footsteps approaching the attic stairs.

I knelt down and hurriedly scooped the envelopes, all of which seemed to be addressed to the Contessa, into a pile, stretching to retrieve one that had landed apart from the rest. To judge from the return addresses, the envelopes contained old business correspondence. In files as neat as I could manage, I restored them to the chest.

I got to my feet and then stood motionless, puzzled. No one had appeared in the attic doorway. No footsteps had mounted the stairs. Yet someone had been in the servants' quarters. Someone still was, unless he had retreated along the hall very quietly indeed. As I listened, I had a distinct sense of someone else straining to listen on the floor below. The sensation was both puzzling and unpleasant.

Unable to reach the shelf, and afraid to use any of the rickety furniture as a stepladder, I hurriedly aligned the leather chest and bronze vase on the floor against the wall. Then I moved to the doorway. Eager as I was to get back to where I belonged, I hesitated there, looking down into the dim hallway. No one stood there, at least not in the length of hall visible to me.

But someone was down there, someplace. I still had that sense of a listening, waiting presence. Nor was it a passive waiting. The dim, musty air seemed charged with some strong emotion–fear? anger? both?–swirling along the hallway and up the staircase to where I stood.

I tried to brush the impression aside. Why should anyone in this household be afraid of me or feel hostility toward me? But the feeling was so strong that it was in something like panic that I hurried down the steep stairs and along the narrow corridor.

A door on my right, just ahead, stood slightly open. Had it been closed when I came along this hall before? I could not remember. I hurried past it, nerves shrinking with the thought that it might suddenly swing wide, that I might hear someone behind me . . .

I heard nothing. But as I moved, almost running, toward the archway, I felt eyes watching me from behind that narrowly opened door.

CHAPTER 7

Down in my room, I stood in the middle of the floor for a few moments, waiting for my pulses to quiet down. I had begun to feel ashamed of myself. Was I, in Caleb's galling phrase, becoming neurasthenic? After all, what had happened up there on the servants' floor? Someone had started to investigate the noise in the attic, and then, for some reason, had changed his mind. Perhaps, I thought, remembering the maid Louisa's unwinking stare, his motive had been sheer Venetian curiosity. From the sound of my voice speaking to Paco, just before the crash of falling objects, he had known who it was up there. He had wanted to observe the American signorina hurrying away, disheveled and embarrassed, from a part of the house where she had no business to be. The idea of stealthily watching eyes was unpleasant, but certainly gave me no reason to feel so disturbed.

I glanced at the traveling clock I had placed on my dressing table. Almost two-thirty. At three I was to give Anna her lessons. There was no time to finish unpacking my trunk, only time to wash my dusty face and hands and change into the blue dimity dress I had planned to wear.

At three I knocked on Anna's door. No doubt reluctant to be set to work under a new taskmistress, she kept me waiting for about half a minute. Then she opened the door and looked up at me with mingled apprehension and defiance.

"Hello, Anna," I said in a brisk let's-have-no-nonsense voice.

She opened the door wider and I stepped past her into the room. It was a child's bedroom, in that the furniture was small-scaled, but otherwise the heavily carved ebony and mahogany echoed the opulence that I had seen in other parts of the house. I looked out onto the balcony and saw, with relief, that Paco was chained to the wrought-iron railing. On the balcony floor stood two clay bowls I assumed to be his dinner plate and water container, and a terra cotta box, with molded vine leaves on its side, which must have once held growing plants. Now it no doubt served to provide for Paco's other necessities.

I thought of telling her about the monkey's theft of my fan. But no, that might increase her hostility toward me. "Well, Anna, shall we begin?"

With obvious reluctance, she led me into a much smaller adjoining room that contained only a long, low table of dark wood, one normal-sized and one child's-sized chair, and a low bookcase. At one end of the table a ball of sculptor's clay rested on an earthen plate. Beside the plate lay the tiny molded figure of a cat. I said, startled, "Did you make that?"

"Yes."

The sculpture was crude and childish, with one ear longer than the other. And yet she had captured the almost boneless appearance of a curled and sleeping cat.

"Have you shown this to the Contessa?"

"No. She wouldn't think it was airsto— airsto—"

"Aristocratic?"

"Yes. Airstocrats don't make pictures and statues. They just order them made."

How dull for the airstocrats, I almost said, but thought better of it. "Where is your history book, Anna?"

The book she brought from the bookcase appalled me. It was an English translation of a history of Venice. A quick glance through it showed me that even a professional historian might find it heavy going. Nevertheless, I handed it to her. "Read to me from where you left off at your last lesson."

Sullenly she began to read, mispronouncing all but the simplest words, an account of a seventeenth-century trade agreement between the Republic of Venice and Verona. I moved to the bookcase and, correcting her pronunciation every few seconds, looked at the other volumes there. A picture book, suitable for a four-year-old. English, French, and Italian grammars. And Gibbon's *Decline and Fall* in English. Her chronic head colds, I decided, must have thickened that Scotswoman's brains.

"Anna, where are books kept in this house?"

The eyes she raised to me held sudden hope. "There's a room near the grand salon."

"Wait here."

In the salon I found Giuseppe, a bolt of scarlet brocade in his arms. He was draping a length of it over a chair back. "What would you think of this for re-covering the chairs? If there's time, I mean, before the ball."

"It's lovely." A thought struck me. "Did you bring that cloth down from the attic?"

"Heavens, no. Nothing goes up there except utterly hopeless junk. I found this in a chest on the ground floor near the kitchen. I hope Grandmother will allow me to hire someone to help with the re-covering. Otherwise I could never get it done in time."

I doubted that Grandmother would. "Is there a library here?"

"There are books, anyway, although I don't know why. No one in this house reads books except Grandmother, and she keeps hers in her room. But you'll find bookcases in an alcove off the card room."

Apparently he had been right about no one reading books. The first one I drew out from the bookcases lining the little alcove was so dusty it made me sneeze. Finally I found something that might do, *Aesop's Fables*, in English. Anna liked animals.

She loved the book. As she read aloud, chortling, about the fox and the grapes, I noticed that now she pronounced easily some of the words she had stumbled over, or pretended to stumble over, only minutes before. When she had read two of the essays, I drilled her in English spelling and Italian grammar, and then went to my room.

At eight, wearing my pale yellow evening dress, I descended the stairs. Apprehension at the thought of facing Caleb again tightened my nerves. But perhaps this would be one of the nights when he dined in a café.

As I crossed the card room toward the dining room, I realized that my clock must have been a little slow, because I could hear Giuseppe's voice and a musical laugh that I knew must be Isabella's. When I entered the room, I saw that Carlo Belzoni was there too, standing with his brother and sister near the far end of the table. With mingled relief and disappointment, I saw that Caleb was not present.

But all three of the women servants were. Louisa and another maid, a thin, plain brunette of middle age, stood flanking the buffet. Maria Rugazzi had stationed herself beside the baize door. Did she always, I wondered, supervise the serving of dinner? Or was she here tonight to honor the homecoming of the eldest male Belzoni?

He came toward me, a smile on his handsome, slightly puffy face, and bent over my hand. "So you took my advice, dear cousin. Welcome to Venice, and to Ca' Belzoni."

I murmured my thanks.

"You will find us a rather nervous household tonight." He laughed. "Grandmother is coming down to dinner. She always does my first night home."

So it was because of the Contessa, rather than the returned grandson, that Maria stood there with that calm, supervisorial look.

Isabella, lovely in a dinner dress of amber-colored silk, smiled at me. "Did you enjoy the Piazza?"

"It was very impressive."

"You didn't stay long. I happened to look out of my window soon after I returned from the puppet show, and I saw you getting out of a gondola, alone."

Her tone was light, but the intentness in her green eyes told me that she was far more interested in Caleb than I had realized that morning. Plainly she had sensed something between Caleb and me, and it had aroused both curiosity and pique.

"I wanted to see if my trunk had arrived."

"Really? Or did you find your old friend dull company? He did say you were old friends, didn't he? At least I—"

She broke off, looking over my shoulder. The Contessa, resplendent in a rich although long-outmoded gown of ivory brocade, was entering the room, carried in Emilio's brawny arms, and with one of her arms encircling his neck. On her head, its thin gray hair now hidden by a luxuriant white wig, rested a narrow diamond tiara. Carried like a prematurely withered infant, she retained every ounce of her formidable dignity.

Giuseppe leaped to draw out a chair at one end of the table. Carefully, the gondolier lowered her into the chair and then, while Giuseppe pushed the chair into place, stepped back to station himself just inside the doorway.

"Sara," the Contessa said, "you will sit beside Carlo at the other end of the table. Isabella and Giuseppe, you will sit at this end."

We took our places. The Contessa unfolded her napkin, and the maids began to circle the table, Louisa holding a big china tureen, and the older maid ladling a clear soup into the bowls of thin, gold-banded china. Maria followed in their wake, filling wine glasses. Seeing the Contessa pick up her spoon, I picked up my own.

It was then that I felt it, the same sensation which had assailed me as I stood at the top of the attic stairs that afternoon. Someone was directing his angry, frightened thoughts at me—someone in this room. It seemed to me that I could sense, as an animal does, that other person's quickened blood, and feel my own pulses speed up in defensive response.

Or was I the object of more than one person's angry fear? Perhaps so, because the emotion I sensed was stronger than the one that had filled that dim top-floor corridor that afternoon, so strong that for a moment I could not raise my eyes. When I did, I saw that my cousins all sat with lowered gaze, spooning their soup. The Contessa, shoulders arrogantly erect, nostrils thinned with some as yet repressed emotion, was also lifting a spoonful of soup. Turning my head slightly, I saw Emilio standing beside the door, arms folded across his broad chest. Against the opposite wall Maria Rugazzi and the two maids stood waiting, their faces expressionless.

I was imagining it, that frightened hostility that amounted to hatred. I must be.

And then the Contessa diverted my attention from everything but herself. Laying down her spoon, she said, "And so. All my surviving grandchildren are gathered here tonight."

She had spoken in English. Why? A moment later I realized why.

"Here is my eldest grandson, a man who travels about the world to put on silly costumes, and bellow preposterous songs from the stage, and spend the money he earns for this nonsense on women, all of them unmarriageable or already married. A man who at thirty-six still shirks his duty to make a good marriage and produce an heir.

"And here is my younger grandson, a man who thinks of himself as artistic, a man who rummages through a chest of fabrics belowstairs like a cabinetmaker's assistant. Oh, yes, I heard about that, Giuseppe.

"And here is my granddaughter, six years married and with no child. A woman who fancies herself the toast of Venice, and yet can't keep her own husband from traveling all over Europe without her."

"I don't choose to go with Enrico," Isabella said. "That much traveling becomes dull."

"Hold your tongue!" the Contessa said. "I know why you like to be separated from your husband. Worthless, worthless, the lot of you."

It was horrible—so horrible that I could not bear to look at any of them. How could she so berate her own grandchildren before me, a stranger? And before the servants, too. Even though they did not understand English, they must have had a good idea, from her scathing tone, of what was going on.

"The only good grandchild was the first-born." Her voice brooded now. "The first to be born, and the first to die. He was a fine soldier. The men of his company adored him. Women adored him, too. He could have married into any of the best families in Venice, and would have, if he had lived. Do you hear that, Carlo? He was a man, my Antonio, and a real Belzoni."

He was also a seducer of servant girls. But perhaps, in this cynical world where I now moved, that was no black mark against him.

The Contessa said in Italian, "I shall go to my room now. Emilio!"

Springing to his feet, Giuseppe drew back her chair. The gondolier stepped forward and lifted her in his arms. Glittering head held high, the terrible old woman was carried from the room.

CHAPTER 8

For a few moments, while I kept my eyes fixed on my soup plate, there was utter silence, not even the click of a spoon. Then Isabella laughed. "Well, that's over for another year!" Apparently careless of the servants, she spoke in Italian. "Comparatively gentle, wasn't she?"

"Especially with you," Carlo said. "Usually she names names. Now I'll have to find out what you've been up to."

Dipping a forefinger into her glass, Isabella flipped wine in his direction. "I don't have to find out about you. It's been in the gossip columns."

Surprised as I was by their gaiety, I was glad of it. I had feared the embarrassment of looking at cowed, scarlet faces. Of the three, only Giuseppe seemed in the least affected. Although he smiled, I could see a small tremor at one corner of his mouth.

"I'm afraid," Carlo said, "that Sara was the real victim of Grandmother's annual auto-da-fé. I looked at you, Sara. You seemed to be wishing that the floor would swallow you."

"Then we shall make it up to her," Isabella said. "I know!" She clapped her hands. "The masquerade ball. I shall have my dressmaker make a beautiful gown for you. She'll take your measurements tomorrow."

"I'm afraid," I said, "that I can't afford a ball gown."

"Silly girl! It will be a present."

"I couldn't accept such a present."

"But you must!" Her voice was urgent. "One night a year Ca' Belzoni relives its ancient splendor. You are a Belzoni connection. People know of your presence here. It would cause talk if you did not appear, and even more talk if you appeared unsuitably dressed." She paused. "My grandmother would be very displeased."

After a moment I said, "Very well then. Thank you."

She waved her hand. "It is nothing. My husband is generous in one respect. He gives me an unlimited clothing allowance."

Giuseppe spoke for the first time since his grandmother had left the room. "He should give more toward the upkeep of this house. It should have been in the marriage contract."

"Isabella felt that wasn't necessary," Carlo said. "She thought she could charm as much money out of him as she wanted."

Isabella smiled sweetly. "Speaking of money, Grandmother plans as usual to invite every heiress in Venice to the ball. And I suppose that, as usual, you will be polite to them, and then arrange a meeting with some trollop like Michele Landi's new wife."

"It should have been in the marriage contract," Giuseppe repeated. "Grandmother should have insisted. She shouldn't have counted on you getting money from Enrico. She keeps talking about the future of the House of Belzoni. I'm the only one who really cares about the house."

Her malice swung toward him. "Don't pretend to be dense, Giuseppe. She's not talking about this house. She means the Belzoni dynasty. And you're not going to help much there, are you?"

It went on like that, all through the roast lamb and vegetables, carried up from somewhere below, all through the fresh strawberries and coffee. I began to wish that Caleb was at the table. Painful as his presence would have been to me, it would at least have afforded me the comfort of seeing in his eyes an echo of my own distaste.

At last Isabella stood up. "Well, what shall we do now? There's a Goldoni comedy at the Fenice. Or would you rather go to the Piazza, Sara? We might run into your American friend there."

I forced a smile. "Perhaps you will. But you must excuse me. I am still tired from my journey."

Carlo protested a little, but only as much as courtesy required. With a sense of release, I moved across the card room and the salon. I did not go to my room. Feeling the need of fresh air, I went down to the ground floor and out the side entrance to the little courtyard. Refracted light from the lantern of Murano glass hanging in the doorway showed me the rectangle of grassy earth set with a young willow, and the marble bench against the wall of the house.

I sat down. I felt lost, completely lost, in this world of heartless cynicism and greed. Far better, I realized now, that I had not fled to my Venetian relatives, but instead used my small funds to support myself in Boston or New York until I found employment.

And Caleb. If I had not crossed the Atlantic, probably I would never have seen Caleb again. Perhaps by now I would have been able to think of him with less bitterness and less longing.

What should I do? Try to borrow money from the Contessa for my passage home? I was sure she would refuse me. I would have to save the money, lira by lira, from the meager wage she had promised me.

Unless, I thought, grimly amused, I could accumulate the needed sum by theft. Among that welter of discarded objects in the attic there were surely a few of some small value. For a moment I indulged myself in a fantasy in which I stole out of the house with a cracked, gilt-framed mirror under my cloak, or a small Cupid with a missing arm, and sold it to some junkdealer.

The attic. That sense of someone's angry fear rising toward me from the dim fourth-floor hall. And tonight, before the Contessa began her tirade, when I had felt that one or more of the persons in the room—one or more of the correctly pleasant-faced family members at the table, one or more of the correctly impassive servants standing against the walls—wore a mask, and from behind that mask stared at me with mingled rage and fear.

I checked my thoughts. Neurasthenia. I must not become neurasthenic. I must hold fast to my Yankee common sense, and to my identity, in this alien world where the beautiful and the bizarre, opulence and decay, exquisite courtesy and cold malice, mingled so strangely.

Think of tomorrow. Perhaps tomorrow I could leave this house and ride out over the still waters of the lagoon to the peace of some tiny, uninhabited island—

A rending sound, somewhere above me. I twisted around on the bench and looked up. Something was hurtling down upon me—something larger than a cannon ball, glimmering pale in the dark.

For a split second I stared, paralyzed, at that onrushing missile. Then I threw myself forward onto the grass. The object struck the bench with an almost explosive sound. Dimly I was aware of something sharp piercing the back of my outspread right hand.

I lay there at full length, hearing the frightened surge of my own blood, for perhaps ten seconds. Then I got shakily to my feet and turned around.

Stone fragments lay scattered on the marble bench and for several feet on the grass in front of it. With a trembling hand I picked up one of the pieces. A stone eye, several times life size, stared up at me balefully from under a half-lowered lid. I looked down. Near my right foot rested a stone ear more than half a foot long.

I put my head back then and looked up. It seemed to me that I could see, just below one of the fourth-floor windows, a dark, roughly circular spot where until minutes ago one of a line of huge stone heads had projected from the wall.

I could have imagined the voiceless threat rising from the dim hall that afternoon and beating at me in the dining room tonight. But these stone fragments were real. With the detachment of shock, I pictured what would have happened if, at the last possible instant, I had not thrown myself forward off the bench. I would be lying there on the grass now, perhaps only blinded or with a pierced jugular vein if the stone head had missed me, but most certainly lifeless if the heavy object had crashed down upon my skull.

My eyes swept along that line of fourth-floor windows—windows of servants' rooms no longer occupied, according to Louisa. No discernible movement up there, and no sound anywhere except the gentle lap of the incoming tide at the landing stage behind me.

That shocked calm dropped away, and my entire body shook. I fled into the house, up the stairs, past the grand salon. No sound but my hurrying footsteps. It was as if the whole vast marble pile had been deserted. But surely the Contessa was here.

I knocked on her door, and her harsh voice bade me come in. Head turned toward the door, she sat in her wheelchair beside the unlighted fireplace. She had been divested of the false hair and the tiara, but she still wore the outmoded ivory satin gown.

"Child! What happened?"

Following the direction of her gaze, I looked down. Blood was oozing from a small cut on the back of my right hand, near the wrist.

"Go in there." She pointed to a door painted in tempera with an oval medallion of a peacock framed by a garland of flowers, which was set in the wall near the fireplace. "Tend to your hand. Then tell me."

Beyond the door I found a dressing room furnished with a washstand, a mirror, and a stately *chaise percée*. Beside the washstand basin stood a small chest of some dark wood inlaid with mother-of-pearl. Inside it I found a roll of linen bandages, a pair of scissors, and a number of vials and bottles. One bottle, according to its label, contained carbolic acid. I washed the cut on my hand—a cut so small I knew that it would be scarcely noticeable by tomorrow—and doused it with carbolic acid. Awkwardly I bandaged it with a length of linen, tearing one end into two strips so that I could tie the bandage in place.

Returning to the bedroom, I sat down at her invitation and told her what had happened. She said in an appalled tone, "You might have been killed."

"I know." Then I blurted out, "I think someone wanted to kill me. I think someone pried that head loose from the wall."

She stared at me as if stunned. "Kill you! Sara, that's nonsense. You are a stranger from across the ocean. You have been in this house less than twenty-four hours. How could anyone have acquired a reason to try to kill you?"

I had no answer.

She said more gently, "You were under strain for months before you came here. And you must find this house and all of us most unsettling. No wonder you have turned—fanciful. But go down to the courtyard in the morning and look up. You will see that two others of the original six heads on that wall have fallen. The other two times, no one was below when the heads fell. This time, you happened to be. Thank God only your hand was hurt."

She fell silent for a moment, looking past my shoulder. "All Venice is falling into decay. Did you know that our city is actually sinking? It was built on hundreds of thousands of piles, driven down through the mud to the clay subsoil. The piles settle another fraction of an inch each year. Already when there is an unusually high tide, the pavement of the Piazza is covered with water."

I gained the impression that there was an odd satisfaction mingled with her melancholy. I could understand it. If the whole city was doomed, what matter that the House of Belzoni had only one small girl to carry on its line?

"Sara, I don't want you to be frightened here, or unhappy. I want you to stay. Anna came to me this evening and read aloud from Aesop. She read beautifully. If only you could have seen her scowling over the book that fool of a Scotswoman assigned to her."

"I did. That's why I substituted Aesop."

"You're good for her, Sara. She likes you. Stay."

"I will." If two of those monstrous heads had fallen in the past, it seemed overwhelmingly probable that only time and gravity had severed the third from the wall. Anyway, I still did not have the money for passage to America.

And besides, how often in her life could Sophia Verracio Belzoni's eyes have held the pleading look I had seen there a moment ago?

"Shall I help you undress?"

"No, I will ring for Maria presently. Go get some sleep now. And in the morning, go for a ride on the lagoon. You're too pale. A few hours of fresh air and sunlight would be good for you."

"I'd like that."

"I will send word to Emilio that he is to take you. Good night, Sara."

As I moved away down the hall, I reflected upon the strange mixture that was my great-aunt. She was stingy, proud, cruel, and sometimes vulgar. Surely if anyone but the Contessa Belzoni had berated her grown grandchildren before a stranger, she would have been considered vulgar. But she could be kind, too. And tonight I had found her pathetic.

I had recovered now from the shock of my near death in the courtyard. And yet before I opened my door, I sent an uneasy glance up the shadowy stairs leading to the fourth floor. Then I went into my room and prepared for bed.

CHAPTER 9

When I emerged into the side courtyard at eight-thirty the next morning, the sun was already uncomfortably warm, giving me a foretaste of the sweltering Venetian summer my grandmother had told me about. I saw that someone had tidied up. No stone fragments littered the bench or the grassy plot.

Tilting my head back, I looked up at the almost circular spot, coated with rough cement, from which that gigantic head had fallen. I looked to my right along the wall and saw a grinning goat's head, and then another circle of rough cement. To the left of the spot from which the head had hurtled down last night was a similar vacant circle, and still farther left the stone head of a mustachioed Turk wearing a cap with a tassel. The last sculpture in the row brought me an unpleasant shock. It was the head and part of the torso of an extremely aged woman, her withered breasts bare. What perverse impulse, I wondered, had caused some long-dead Belzoni to have that symbol of bodily decay placed upon his palace wall?

From my left came the sound of an opening door. Emilio stepped from an archway, a low, narrow one that probably led to the kitchen and laundry room. The gondolier carried a large wooden bucket with a rope handle. At sight of me he stopped short and then said, "Good morning, signorina."

"Good morning. I'm ready to go out on the lagoon now." Then, at the disconcerted look on his swarthy face: "Didn't the Contessa send word to you?"

"Yes, but I didn't expect you so early."

I said, beginning to feel annoyed, "Well, I'm here."

"I was intending to go over to one of the islands to empty eel traps. Perhaps when I get back—"

"It will be too hot by that time. I'll go with you over to the island."

"And ride back in the gondola with eels, signorina?"

"Eels don't bother me." Often my father and I had gone eeling and crabbing in the brackish waters bordering Long Island Sound.

"It is an uninteresting island. No one ever goes there."

Thoroughly irritated now, I said, "Well, I choose to."

I saw a flicker of answering anger in his eyes. Then, as if a sudden thought had occurred to him, he smiled. "Very well, signorina."

Half an hour later we had left the Grand Canal's busy traffic of gondolas and fruit-and-vegetable-laden barges, glided past the church of Santa Maria della Salute with its balloonlike dome, and were out on the placid, sun-dazzled waters of the lagoon. Emilio seemed to have lost his sullenness. From the rower's stand behind me, he pointed out the island of Murano, where for centuries Venetian glassblowers had twisted crystalline bubbles into shapes both beautiful and bizarre, and the cemetery island of San Michele, and, in the distance, the almost deserted island of Torcello, which had been more populous than Venice itself until the inhabitants began to flee its malarial plagues.

"And how," Emilio asked, "do you like Venice?"

"I find it strange and beautiful."

"It is more than that. They come here on their wedding journeys, the French, the Germans, the English. Even some rich Americans. And why? Because the nights of Venice are made for love."

I ignored that. "What is the name of this island we are going to?"

"Santa Theodosia. There was a monastery on it hundreds of years ago. Now there are only ruins—and eels in the ditches. Tell me, what do you think of Signorina Isabella? A very lively young lady, no? And Signore Giuseppe. How does he strike you?"

Not liking the tenor of his questions, I said shortly, "I find him pleasant."

"So? I do not. I find him a joke, one that grows less funny. Always he is pestering me to pose for him in the gondola. Someday I will throw him into the Grand Canal."

I twisted around so that I could see him there, one foot advanced, brawny arms poised to lunge forward with the long oar. "If you don't stop that sort of talk, I shall tell the Contessa."

He completed the stroke before he said, "I think you won't. I think you are not a talebearer."

"Don't be too sure," I said, and faced forward again. He rowed in silence after that, but I had an uneasy feeling that it was a satisfied, rather than a cowed, silence.

We were heading for a low, flat island now, treeless except for a few small poplars. I could see the broken, reddish clay walls of a fairly large building which must have been the monastery, and several smaller buildings, also in ruins.

Emilio moored the gondola to a weathered pole at one end of a wooden landing platform. After lifting the bucket out of the boat, he extended his hand to me. With his aid, I stepped onto the platform. Then, as if I had stumbled, which I had not, he grasped my upper arms.

I said, "If you don't let go of me this instant, I certainly will tell the Contessa."

His hands dropped from my arms, but he did not step back. "Why? I know. It is because I am poor, and a servant."

I said, with an uneasy feeling that he might be partly right, "That has nothing to do with it."

"It should not. After all, you too are poor and paid wages by the Contessa, just like me. Besides, what if I should grow rich someday soon? What then, eh?"

I realized that he was motivated less by amorousness than a desire to disconcert me. But I also sensed that he was half in earnest.

"Emilio, I've warned you."

He stepped back. "Very well, signorina. Shall I show the signorina over the island?"

"The signorina will show herself over the island."

I stepped off the low platform onto a narrow path that ran through the high grass and walked away, aware that his gaze followed me.

I looked into the largest of the ruined buildings first. The wood of its wide door frame was rotten, and the doors themselves missing. Sunlight, falling through holes in the roof, showed me a rubble-choked aisle between two rows of doorless cells. Apparently the rear part of the building had collapsed entirely, because through an archway at the end of the aisle I could see nothing but a welter of fallen beams and broken plaster.

About thirty feet farther along the path I found the remains of a round building which must have been the chapel, because opposite the doorway there was a small alcove where an altar could have been placed. It must have been a very poor monastery. The chapel floor was not of marble or of rich mosaics like that of St. Mark's, but of eight-sided tiles of varying sizes, joined by broken mortar, and so faded with age that it was impossible to tell whether their original color had been dark red, or brown, or even some other shade.

But the humble place had not been without ornament. Through the broken roof sunlight slanted onto a mosaic that curved along the little alcove's wall. Stepping gingerly over broken and loosened tiles, I crossed the chapel for a closer look. Patches of mosaic had vanished, revealing the red clay wall beyond, but enough remained so I could make out a sad-eyed Madonna and a Child with that prematurely aged, Byzantine look.

Leaving the chapel, I peered into what might have been an ancient kitchen—an ovenlike dome, still largely intact, stood against one wall—and then into a building that undoubtedly had housed sheep or cattle. Plainly this building had been in use at a far more recent time than the days when cowled monks knelt in the chapel. Here not all of the wood had fallen into dust or been carted away for firewood. Four stalls, although obviously rotten, still stood along one wall. There was a loft for the storage of hay, and even a rickety ladder leading up to it. Not too many years ago, apparently, a farmer on the mainland or some other island of the lagoon had used Santa Theodosia for pasturage.

Leaving the cluster of long-silent buildings, I followed the path through grass that grew steadily taller, until it was almost waist-high, to the other side of the island. The high tide, covering whatever beach there might have been, gnawed at the soft, grassy soil. Even as I watched, thimble-sized chunks of earth were torn away to melt in the water. If Venice had been constructed on similar soil, I could well understand why its builders needed first to drive foundation piles down to the firmer clay.

Surely Emilio had collected his eels by now. I retraced my steps past the cattle shed and the ancient kitchen. I could see Emilio on the landing stage now, back turned to me as, with the wooden bucket in his hand, he looked down into the gondola. At the doorway of the chapel I paused to glance in at the Byzantine Madonna and Child. To my surprise, I saw large, muddy footprints leading over the broken tile to the alcove and then back to the doorway. Obviously Emilio, after fetching his eels from some brackish inlet, had paid a visit to the crumbling mosaic. Until now he had not struck me as a man who would take the time to pay tribute to some long-dead artist's creation left to crumble away on this deserted island. But apparently I had been wrong. And perhaps poor Giuseppe was right. Perhaps Emilio was "a remarkable person, quite above his station."

I found that the idea made me like him no better.

I moved toward the landing platform. He was on his knees now, stowing the bucket in the gondola. He got to his feet and, at the sound of my skirts swishing through the grass, turned to face me.

"Are you ready to go back now, Emilio?"

He said with an exaggerated air of humility, "Whatever the signorina wishes."

He helped me into the gondola, relinquishing my hand with correct promptitude. In correct silence, he rowed me back to Venice. The only sound was that made by the eels sloshing around in their bucket a few inches from the toes of my shoes.

CHAPTER 10

As THE GONDOLA glided to a stop at the side entrance to the Belzoni house, I saw, with a leap of my pulses, that Caleb was crossing the courtyard toward me. It was he, not Emilio, who helped me to the landing stage. Feeling a tingle run up my arm as his hand briefly clasped mine, I wondered if a time would ever come when I would not be stirred by even the slightest touch of this man. He said, "Did you enjoy your trip on the lagoon?"

"Yes. How did you know where I'd gone?"

"Isabella told me. She saw you leave, and so she asked the Contessa about it."

Isabella. The first time he mentioned her to me he had called her Signora Ponzi. "Did you run into Isabella and her brothers in the Piazza last night?"

"Yes. I spent some time with them and then went off to the Café Guardia."

However brief that "some time" had been, apparently it had been long enough for him and Isabella to reach a first-name basis.

Emilio lifted the bucket of eels from the gondola. "Is there anything else, signorina?"

"No." After a moment I added, "Thank you."

"Then good day, signorina, signore."

Caleb looked after him as he walked toward the low doorway. "Has that fellow been presumptuous?"

"It was nothing I couldn't cope with." I paused. "How did you guess?"

"Your face. And his. He was being far too much the humble servitor. If he'd been an English plowman, he'd have pulled his forelock." He paused. "If he gives you any more trouble, let me know. I'll handle him."

I said, after a moment, "Then you still intend to stay here?"

"I'll go back to London if you insist. I decided that last night at the Guardia, over more brandies than were good for me."

I was silent for several moments, and then said, "I don't insist. I have no right to. I don't own Venice or the Belzoni house."

"In that case, I'll tell you something else I decided last night. I decided to suggest that we treat each other just as friends and compatriots who happen to be here at the same time. I know this city, and I love it. I would like to show it to you in a way that would make you enjoy it.

"You can trust me," he went on. "I'll never again ask you to change your mind about me. And I'll never refer to the past."

I weighed the suggestion. My instinct was to save myself pain by avoiding him. But that would be hard to do while he stayed under the Belzoni roof. Certainly it would be less awkward if we could treat each other merely as friends. Perhaps before too long the pretense would begin to seem real to me. Perhaps by the time he left for London, his departure would bring me less relief, and less regret, than otherwise would have been the case.

I forced a smile. "Very well. We're friends."

"Fine. Will you allow a friend to take you to lunch? In about an hour, say? We could meet at the public landing stage."

"All right." I would have time to change from my shirtwaist and blue cotton walking skirt to something more suitable. "In an hour."

I had been in my room only a few minutes when someone

knocked. Before I could answer, Isabella's voice called, "Are you back, Sara?"

I opened the door. A woman stood beside my cousin—a thin, middle-aged brunette whose cowed expression, as well as the bolt of white cloth in her arms and the paper of pins affixed to the bosom of her black dress, told me that she was Isabella's dressmaker.

"This is Signora Marcuttio, Sara. She has come to take your measurements for your ball gown."

As soon as they were inside the room, Isabella took the bolt of cloth from the dressmaker's arms and flung a length of it along the bed. The material was gauzy white silk, shimmering, almost transparent, and obviously expensive.

"Isn't it beautiful? And here is how it will look." Reaching into the bosom of her dress, she took out a piece of paper and unfolded it. It bore a colored print of a woman in the sort of gown worn about a hundred years ago.

"See? I tore this out of one of those old books down in the card room. You will be a grand lady at Napoleon's court. That high waistline will give you more bosom. And with your hair dressed high like that, your neck will look longer. I'll loan you a pearl necklace to wear with it. They're not real, but that won't matter, not for a masquerade.

"Some of the old dowagers won't like your costume," she rattled on. "They can't forgive Napoleon for handing us over to Austria. But who cares about them! Why, the Austrian occupation has been over for fifteen years!"

Tilting her red-gold head to one side, she smiled roguishly and added, "Of course, Napoleon's sister and some of the other ladies wore nothing at all under their gowns, but I don't suppose you will want to go that far."

"No, not that far."

White is not my best color. And if I had to have a gown for a masquerade ball, I could have preferred the sort of graceful, flowing costume worn, with a high peaked hat, by medieval ladies. But I was the recipient, however unwilling, of a gift, and one does not criticize a gift.

From the pocket of her dress the seamstress drew a tape measure. I removed my shirtwaist and skirt and stood there in my petticoat and camisole while the woman took my measurements. "You look somewhat impatient, Sara. Were you planning to go somewhere?"

"Yes, I have an appointment."

"With Caleb Hayworth?"

Perhaps if I had looked up while Caleb and I stood down there on the landing stage, I would have seen Isabella watching us from some window. Which, I wondered, was her room? On this floor there were ten rooms, including the Contessa's and Anna's and mine, on this side of the house, and presumably an equal number on the other side of the open space above the grand salon's copper roof, as well as additional rooms at the rear.

"Yes," I said, "with Caleb Hayworth. By the way, Isabella, where is your room?"

"Two doors from Grandmother's."

"And Carlo's and Giuseppe's?"

"Across the court. But don't try to change the subject. We were talking about Caleb. What a coincidence that you two should be old friends."

"Not really. He is a teacher. So was my father. That's how we met."

"Oh, Sara! You know what I mean. It's coincidence that you two should be here."

I swallowed my annoyance at this none-too-subtle inquisition. After all, she was being generous. Heaven knew how much she was paying for my gown. Certainly its cost would be the equivalent of many months of my salary here. "He has always traveled a lot, and Venice is a favorite city of his."

"Sara, Sara!" Her teasing smile flashed. "You're evading. But I give you fair warning. I intend to try to bedazzle your tall American."

"In that case," I said, trying to make my voice as light as hers, "the poor man doesn't have a chance."

She and the dressmaker left, finally, taking the bolt of filmy, precious stuff with them. Hurriedly, I dressed to meet Caleb.

He took me to a restaurant that overlooked a half-mile-wide channel, with that strip of land known as the Giudecca forming its other shore. From our tree-shadowed table in a little courtyard, we could see across blue water to the mass of ships anchored along the bank, and to the domes and bell towers of several churches beyond. We ate white, delicate fish caught in the lagoon that morning, and sipped a white wine from the Po Valley. And Caleb told me anecdotes about Lord Byron, who about sixty years before had lived in a Venetian palace along with fourteen indolent and thieving servants and a menagerie which included a mastiff, a wolf, and a fox, all ill-tempered. But the most fierce member of that strange household, Caleb said, was Byron's latest mistress, a baker's Amazonian wife who, once brought to the house, refused to leave. At last, infuriated by the poet's insistence that she leave, she stabbed him in the thumb with a table knife, was disarmed by his servants, and ran out to the Grand Canal and jumped in.

"Did she drown?"

"No. They pulled her out. Byron sent for a doctor and stood by while she was resuscitated. I imagine he was quite calm about it. He'd had a lot of experience with feminine suicide attempts."

"Did he take her back?"

"No. And perhaps that dive in the canal had cooled some of her passion for him. Anyway, she went home."

It was time, I told him regretfully, that I do the same. At three I was to give Anna her lessons.

"How about tomorrow afternoon? I'm going to look at some seventeenth-century account books in a shop in the Old Ghetto. Would you like to join me there afterwards?"

The Old Ghetto. Shylock and Jessica and the three caskets. "I'd love it."

"Good. We'll meet at a café I know at five o'clock. That will give us plenty of time to look around before dinner." Taking a map from his jacket pocket, he said, "The easiest way for you to get there is on foot."

With a pencil he traced a route over footbridges and across little squares and through curving streets. "Think you can remember that? Or do you want the map?"

"I can remember, and if I don't, I can always ask someone."

As a public gondola carried us back to Ca' Belzoni, I reflected that he had kept his word. Throughout that luncheon he had behaved as a friend and entertaining host. From his manner no one would have guessed that we had ever stood locked in each other's arms, or stabbed each other with words in the shade-dimmed living room of a Connecticut house.

It seemed a pity that, mingled with my relief at his friendly, impersonal attitude, there was a distinct sense of loss.

Seven hours later, after I had given Anna her lessons, after a protracted dinner during which Isabella flirted with Caleb—meaning it—and Carlo Belzoni had flirted with me—not meaning it—I went to the Contessa's room.

When I had helped her into the gilded bed and measured out her sleeping draft, she asked, "Did you visit any of the islands in the lagoon today?"

"Just one, Santa Theodosia."

"Oh, yes. Where Emilio keeps his eel traps."

"They were sad, all those ruined buildings, but I loved them, particularly the little chapel."

"I remember it. When I was young, we often had picnics on Santa Theodosia. Of course, no one but Emilio ever goes there now."

"So he told me. But he didn't say why."

"Emilio has threatened to beat up any other eel fisherman who sets foot there. And the snakes keep everyone else away."

"Snakes!"

"Oh, not around that cluster of old buildings. They keep to

the high grass at the other end of the island. Still, no one wants to take a chance. The snakes are vipers, and very poisonous."

And without a word of warning, Emilio had watched me walk away toward that waist-high grass. Well, since nothing had happened to me, I wouldn't tell the Contessa about it. But from now on I would have as little as possible to do with him.

She asked, "Is that old mosaic still in the chapel?"

"Yes. I loved it. Even Emilio seems attracted to it, although he must have seen it often. After he collected his eels, he went into the chapel to look at it. I saw his muddy footprints on the floor."

My great-aunt snorted. "If Emilio visited the mosaic, it wasn't out of any religious or artistic sentiment. He was up to no good. Perhaps he's trying to figure out some way of getting it loose from the wall, so he can sell it in the Rialto. There are shops there that handle antiquities. Open the draperies, Sara."

I drew back the draperies at the long windows, which stood open on this warm night. "You'd better close the windows nearest my bed," the Contessa said. "It may grow chilly by morning."

I reached out onto the balcony and grasped the window's wrought-iron handle. At that moment a voice singing "Celeste Aïda," a voice I had last heard filling the Metropolitan Opera House, rose into the night. I looked down. A gondola, with Emilio wielding the long oar, glided around the corner of Ca' Belzoni and into the Grand Canal. Light cast by the entryway lantern showed me Carlo's flung-back head, and Giuseppe's curly dark one, and Caleb's brown-blond one. Isabella sat beside Caleb, the red-gold glint of her hair visible through a gossamer-thin white shawl.

They were going, probably, to the Piazza, where the band would be playing, and the Venetian young would be strolling in their finery, and the sound of talk and laughter and clinking glasses would rise from the tables set out in the vast square.

No one, not even Caleb, had suggested that I accompany them.

It was just as well. Better that we confine our association to the daylight hours. In the soft Venetian nights, Caleb might forget that now we were just friends and compatriots, and I might want him to forget it.

Behind me the Contessa said, "My grandson, isn't it? Bellowing a silly song into the night like some public gondolier!"

I closed the window and turned toward her. "Yes, it was Carlo. I imagine they're all going to the Piazza."

Perhaps there was something forlorn in my face, because she said, "Come here, Sara. Bend down."

I obeyed. Her dry lips touched my cheek. When I straightened, she said, "Keep as aloof as possible from my grandchildren. And keep to the standards of your dowdy old queen. Otherwise you may find Venice a very treacherous bog indeed."

CHAPTER 11

Around five the next afternoon, I was moving through a city that had become eerie and dreamlike, its sounds muffled, its little squares and narrow streets filled with fog that was sometimes opalescent, as if the sun were about to break through, and sometimes a thick gray smother.

I had first noticed the fog gathering outside the long dining room windows while I shared a cold buffet luncheon with the Contessa's grandchildren. When I exclaimed over it, Carlo smiled and said, "You're surprised at fog in a city surrounded by water? Sometimes it's so thick that no traffic moves along the canals."

I thought of my five o'clock appointment with Caleb. Perhaps by then the fog would have lifted.

Holding a bunch of grapes in one narrow white hand, Isabella said, "You look troubled. Were you planning to go out today?"

"Yes. I wanted to see the Old Ghetto."

"With Caleb?"

"Yes. We're meeting at a café near there after I've given Anna her lessons."

Her smile looked amused. Her eyes did not. "Scarcely a day for sightseeing, I would say."

"That only proves you have no imagination," Giuseppe said.

"Even if you can't see details, Venice is marvelous in a fog, mysterious and exciting."

She turned that smile on him. "Perhaps to you. But you forget how different you are from most people." Through his waspish answer, I murmured an excuse and retreated to my room.

The weather did not clear. When I finally left the house—after a session with the dressmaker and after Anna's lessons—fog shrouded the courtyard and the walkway that led from the Belzoni landing stage to a bridge spanning the side canal. Giuseppe had been right. It was exciting, in an eerie way, to move along the narrow walk, with a row of *palazzos,* their upper floors lost in mist, on my right, and on my left a canal that had become a river of curdled milk, with the water showing black through an occasional rent.

I crossed the bridge. Following the route I had committed to memory, I moved along a narrow street, cut diagonally across a little square, where an orange cat slunk so closely across my path that I almost stumbled over him, and entered another street, equally narrow. Venetians, apparently, regarded the waning hours of a fog-bound day as a good time to stay indoors. Except for the cat and a little old woman who had passed me like a bent black shadow, I had encountered no one since leaving the Belzoni house.

I crossed a second bridge, moved a few yards along a street, and then into a square where I could barely make out two figures standing beside a well head. To judge from the low murmur of their voices, they were a man and a woman, both young. On the other side of the square I entered a street so narrow that, by stretching out my arms, I almost could have touched opposite house fronts. Here the eaves shut out nearly all the mist-filtered daylight, so that the fog became a dark gray smother.

I had gone only a few yards over the street's fog-slippery paving stones when I became aware of them—following footsteps, not quite synchronized with mine. Some instinct made me halt. I heard a single footfall, and then silence.

My heart gave a nervous leap. Did the silence mean that he had turned into some doorway? Or was he still back there, waiting to follow as soon as I moved on? I strained my ears. No sound but the drip of moisture from overhanging eaves and the muffled peal of church bells somewhere nearby, ringing vespers. If he was still there, who was he? Some thief, bent upon robbing anyone foolish enough to venture out into this smother?

And then, unbidden, a sickening memory flashed across my mind—that gigantic head, hurtling down like a cannon ball toward me through the darkness. If it had struck me, I would have been deemed the victim of an accident. And if I were discovered minutes or hours from now, lying clubbed or stabbed on the wet pavement, my death would be attributed to some unknown criminal.

Stop it, I told myself sternly. True, I had told my cousins where I was going, and I had told Anna, who in turn could have told someone else. But no one from the Belzoni household was back there behind that sluggishly eddying gray curtain. What reason could any of them have to stalk me through the concealing fog?

No one at all was there. He had turned into some house.

Or had he? Under cover of the bells and the steady drip of moisture, had he moved closer, so that in a moment I would see . . . ?

And then it seemed to me I did see it, a dim shape taking form, a darker gray against the grayness.

I turned, heart pounding, and moved as swiftly as I dared over the treacherous paving stones. I felt a scream welling in my throat. But I must not scream. A scream might bring him in a rush to strike me down and then fade swiftly back into the thick smother. Better to keep moving until I saw a lighted shop window. But there seemed to be no shops at all along this street. And if there were lights beyond the house windows, shuttered against the damp, they were invisible to me.

I could hear the footsteps again. Not running footsteps. Evidently he, too, did not trust the wet pavingstones. But now, as if aware that I knew he followed, he made no attempt to synchronize his steps with mine. And he was closer. Much closer. Stomach knotted with panic, I fought down the impulse to dart to a door and pound on the panels. Long before anyone could answer, he could be upon me, bringing a club down upon my head or thrusting a knife between my shoulder blades.

The hurrying steps were very close now, perhaps only five or six yards behind me. There was no help for it. I ran, trying not to think of how I might slip and lie helpless, watching my assailant—nameless, faceless, sexless, and all the more terrifying for that—rush toward me out of the fog.

At the end of the street I emerged into a square filled with the muffled sound of bells somewhere to my left. I saw a well head in time to avoid colliding with it, ran the rest of the way across the square, and entered a narrow street, bumping shoulders with a short, stocky man who muttered "Scusa" in a surprised voice and moved aside. I went on, still running, but with my fear ebbing now. Ahead, looming through the fog, I could see dim light which surely emanated from the café Caleb had mentioned.

It did. For a moment before I opened the door, I looked to my left. Nothing. Nothing beyond the loom of the light except heavy gray mist moving in sluggish eddies between the house fronts.

I went into the café, into the blessed glow of gas lamps, and the sight of curious faces turning and of Caleb hurrying toward me. I saw his expression change.

"What happened?"

"Someone was following me."

He did not say I must have imagined it, as I had feared he would. "You shouldn't have been out alone. Weather like this makes a field day for petty criminals. About four-thirty I thought of going back to the house to keep you from coming, but the fog thinned a little just then, and I figured it might clear."

I thought of saying that perhaps it was not some petty criminal. But I feared reading that word "neurasthenic" in his eyes. Besides, now that I was with Caleb, now that I was safe, it seemed overwhelmingly probable to me that the pursuer had been some pickpocket or—an unpleasant idea, but even less alarming—some doorway lounger who had glimpsed a young woman abroad in this unlikely weather, and had drawn the wrong conclusion about her.

With his hand on my elbow, Caleb led me toward a table. "No sightseeing today. We'll have a glass of something, and then go back to Ca' Belzoni."

CHAPTER 12

DURING THE NEXT two weeks, Ca' Belzoni was readied for its annual night of renewed glory, the masquerade ball. I observed to my surprise that the Contessa, although she never left her room, directed all but the minor details of those preparations. At her orders, relayed by Maria Rugazzi, additional servants were hired, a certain orchestra engaged, and French rather than Italian champagne ordered. To Giuseppe's delight, she even decreed that all the picture frames in the grand salon were to be regilded, and the missing prisms in the chandelier replaced. "As you pointed out," he said to me, "that worn upholstery won't show up much at night, but those missing prisms made a dreadful effect."

Except for standing patiently while Isabella's dressmaker fitted and refitted my white gown, I took no part in all this activity. I gave Anna her lessons each afternoon. Each night, if the Contessa so desired, I read to her for an hour after dinner. Otherwise I was free to wander with Caleb through Venice.

When only a few days had passed, I found that my perception of the city had changed. The Venetian love of fine clothes, which at first had struck me as foolishly ostentatious, now seemed to me pleasant, even praiseworthy. There was something touchingly gallant about these people moving with graceful assurance across the Piazza and along the narrow streets. After the long decline of its commerce and its humiliating occupation by Austria,

Venice was now one of the poorer cities of a newly united Italy. But from the proud air of its citizens, even the poor people, one might have thought that this was still the Republic of Venice, its armies victorious on almost every field, and its ambassadors received with sometimes fawning respect in all the courts of Europe.

We went back to St. Mark's, and this time I looked around me with more appreciative and more tolerant eyes. Why shouldn't the Venetians, especially in the vainglorious Middle Ages, have poured out their riches and the talents of their painters and goldsmiths and sculptors to house the body of their patron saint—stolen, it was true, but at great peril, and therefore all the more venerated.

But it was not glittering St. Mark's, or the smaller churches with their radiant Titians and Tintorettos, or the proud old houses along the canals, that filled me with a growing delight. It was small things. A canary's cage, hung out of a window above a narrow street, so that the bird could enjoy the sunlight, and passers-by his song. A tiny little shrine recessed in a garden's outer wall, with one rosebud in a vase from a child's toy china set placed before an eight-inch-high Virgin. The innumerable little squares—still called *campi,* because hundreds of years ago they had actually been fields—where often as not an old public well stood, with a few of Venice's myriad cats asleep on its coping. And almost always during those morning hours, or the hours between the end of Anna's lessons and dinnertime, Caleb was with me, pointing out a graceful archway or carved window pediment that otherwise I might have missed, and regaling me with stories from a thousand years of Venetian history, until the past as well as the present seemed to take on a dazzling richness.

What matter that at night while I was reading aloud to the Contessa, or to myself in my room, Caleb was out somewhere with my cousins? I was sure that I enjoyed my daylight hours more than they enjoyed their evenings, and that Caleb, too, probably had a better time during our wanderings.

One evening near the dinner hour, as a gondola carried us toward the Belzoni house, we glided toward an arched footbridge which spanned the narrow canal. Affixed to the highest point of the arch was a bronze bas-relief, greenish with age, of a naked, laughing little boy with a dolphin in his arms. The dolphin, one felt, was not his captive, but his playmate. The water, shimmering like shot silk in the sunset light, reflected the two frolicking creatures.

Tears of sheer delight came to my eyes. I felt that never since that bridge was built had boy and dolphin and sunset-dyed water been in such harmony. I wanted to fix the instant in time and hold it close, as the boy held the dolphin.

Something hard and knotted gave way inside me, and I knew that I was happy. What was more, I knew why I was happy, and why these past few days I had looked at everything, from the golden glitter of St. Mark's to a sleeping stray cat, through different eyes.

Venice was a city for lovers. And these past days the man I loved had been beside me. He was beside me now.

A man stubbornly true to his lights, he had done what he had done to my father and, as he had told me, would do it again if he had to. Well, at last I could accept that. Bitterness could not restore my father's life, any more than grief could. It could only cost me happiness with the one man I might ever love.

I wanted to turn to him right there, in front of the gondolier who was rowing us closer and closer to the Belzoni house. But no, even if there had been time, that would not have been the way to do it. The breach between us was too wide and deep to be closed by a look, a few words. Better to go on without words for a little while, drawing closer and closer, as we had been, and as Caleb must have known we would. In a few days—three, or four, or five—he would turn to me, and we would find we were so close that we need not even take back my bitter charges and his unyielding answers. The wounds we had dealt each other in that Connecticut house would have healed almost without trace.

The gondola left us at the Belzoni house. As we crossed the landing stage, Caleb said, "I'm going to Padua tomorrow. The Contessa asked me to, through the housekeeper. I imagine I won't be back until late in the evening."

"To Padua? What for?"

"To order some champagne. The local wine sellers were out of the vintage she wanted, so she sent back what they did deliver. And time is growing short. The ball is next Thursday."

I said as we entered the house, "I suppose Carlo refused to go, and she wouldn't trust Giuseppe to."

He laughed. "Either that, or she's heard those stories about hard-headed Yankees and thinks I'll make a better deal."

When we reached the door of my room, he said, "Day after tomorrow, let's go over to the Lido. We can leave early, with a picnic lunch, and be back in time for Anna's lessons."

The Lido. According to Carlo, big luxury hotels for foreigners might soon be erected on the lagoon's barrier beach. But now it was probably much the same lovely wilderness my grandmother had described.

Caleb and I, alone among the palmettos and wild roses. "I'd like that."

"Fine. Let's meet at the public landing stage at ten day after tomorrow. See you at dinner," he said, and turned toward the stairs.

That evening, while I read *Barchester Towers* in Italian to the Contessa, and all the next day while I stood for the final fitting of my gown and gave Anna her lessons, I felt lightheaded with happiness. That happiness must have been both obvious and becoming, because at dinner Carlo looked at me with what, for the first time, seemed genuine interest, and Isabella's eyes regarded me with a certain thoughtfulness in their green depths.

After dinner Carlo suggested that I go with them to the

theater, and Isabella—I suppose because Caleb was absent—seconded his invitation. I pleaded a headache. I wanted to be alone in my room hugging my happiness to me. I wanted to wait until I heard Caleb's footsteps pass my door. On two previous nights, when I happened to be wakeful, I had heard his footsteps at some time after midnight. I had not opened my door, of course. But tonight I might step out into the hall and ask him about his trip to Padua.

I helped the Contessa to bed, glad that tonight she did not want to be read to, and measured out her sleeping draft. Then I went to my room. Because I was waiting for Caleb, I did not undress. I sat in my room's one chair reading *The Stones of Venice,* with only an occasional word or phrase registering upon my mind.

Eleven-thirty passed, midnight, twelve-thirty. Well, he had said he would be late. But at one o'clock I gave up. I undressed and extinguished the light. Then, still wakeful, I put my robe on over my nightdress and stepped out onto the balcony.

I had not realized there was a full moon. Its radiance turned the white wall of the garden opposite to silver-blue. It glistened on the glossy leaves of an ilex that raised its head above the wall, so that the tree seemed hung with bluish lights, and it flung a silver ribbon down the center of the canal. Giddy with joy and moonlight, I leaned far out over the rail, trying to see the bridge where the little boy embraced the dolphin. I could not. A bend in the canal intervened.

I straightened. Then, somewhere to my left, I heard Isabella's soft laugh. Instinctively I shrank back into the shadows.

Her glorious hair down around her shoulders, and in a peignoir of some light shade—it was impossible to tell the exact color in that deceptive moonlight—she stood on the balcony of her room, her back to the railing.

"Come on out here!" Low as her voice was, it carried through the still night. I heard someone in her room give an indistinct reply.

"Nonsense! Who would be awake at this hour? Say good night to me out here in the moonlight."

As my thudding heart and shrinking nerves had known he would, Caleb stepped out onto the balcony, tall in white shirt sleeves and dark trousers. She went into his arms, and they kissed, and he murmured something into her ear. Then, with his arm around her waist, they went back into her room.

I stumbled into my own room. Not the first time, I thought; not the first time. Her manner had lacked the shyness that even an Isabella must feel at the outset of an intrigue. And as they stepped back into the room, there had been something practiced and proprietary in the way his arm encircled her waist.

All these days, while he showed me Titians behind the altars of dim churches and regaled me with anecdotes from Venice's long past, he must have been anticipating the hour when he would go to Isabella's room.

In the Piazza the day after my arrival, I had said that I felt Venice was a masked carnival. He had implied that I was becoming neurasthenic. But people in Venice did wear masks. Especially Caleb.

When I heard his footsteps, I did not move out into the hall. I could not have even if I had desired to, because I felt too numb and sick to rise from my bed.

CHAPTER 13

A LITTLE BEFORE ten the next morning, I stood waiting for Caleb at the public landing stage. All through a sleepless night I had debated with myself. Should I send him a scathing note? No, I finally decided, I would confront him. I wanted to see his face as I denounced his lechery, his cruel hypocrisy.

He was moving toward me along the narrow walkway that ran between the Belzoni entryway and the public landing stage. In one hand he carried a wicker basket—that picnic lunch for our sun-drenched hours amid the wild roses of the Lido.

He said, "You got here early, I see." Then, in a changed tone: "What's wrong? You look ill."

"I didn't sleep."

He did not ask why. I sensed that already he had guessed. "Perhaps you can take a nap when we get to the Lido."

"I don't want to go there."

He said after a moment, "All right." He turned to one of the waiting gondoliers, a middle-aged man we had frequently hired. "Francesco, will you please give this basket to the Belzoni cook?"

When the man had walked away, Caleb asked, "Do you want to go somewhere else?"

"Yes. Someplace where we can talk."

"All right. Where?"

Yes. Where? Where in Venice, this loathsome city, could one conduct a conversation such as ours would be? The streets were so narrow that other pedestrians, including any who spoke English, would hear you. The cafés were not open yet. In a gondola your every word was audible to the gondolier. True, most churches would be deserted at this hour, but a church scarcely seemed the proper setting.

"The little park," I said finally, "near that restaurant on the Giudecca Channel."

"All right." Now his tone, like his bony face, was expressionless.

In silence we waited until the gondolier, Francesco, returned. He rowed us to the channel's north bank. There we climbed steps to a narrow strip of grassy land set with flower beds and with a line of marble benches bordering a path. We sat down, facing the blue water. The only other people in the little park at this hour were a nursemaid, sitting on a bench some sixty feet away, and her small charges, both girls, who rolled a hoop along the path.

"All right. Let's have it."

I looked at a three-masted schooner angling toward a dock on the other side of the channel. "I saw you and Isabella on the balcony last night."

"So that's it. I thought so."

"And last night wasn't the first time you'd been in her room, was it?"

"No. It was the seventh or eighth. I'm not sure which."

I turned upon him. His gaze was following the schooner. "Is that all you have to say about your adultery?"

He still watched the schooner. "It's adultery for her. It's only fornication for me. I'm not married."

"How vile you are!"

He turned to me then. "What did you expect? I came to Venice hoping you would throw yourself in my arms. You didn't. There'd been no sea change. You still felt as you did in Connecticut. You even told me to go back to London. It wasn't until I promised to treat you just as a friend that you seemed reconciled to my staying."

"A friend! You betrayed me."

"How did I betray you? Would you have opened the door of your room to me?"

"Of course not."

"Yes, of course not. Nor would you marry me. But here was a woman who had made it clear almost from the moment we met that she was willing as well as beautiful."

"That's no excuse for lechery."

"Oh, Sara, Sara! Don't you understand anything? I'd never have touched her if you'd said what I'd hoped you'd say the night you arrived here. And so I ask you again, where is the betrayal?"

I wanted to say, You betrayed me with kindness and gentleness these past few days. You betrayed me by making me love you more than ever.

Instead I said, "Until last night I thought that perhaps you still loved me."

He sounded tired. "I do, but I don't expect you to believe that. Maybe it's not your fault. It's the way women are raised in England and America in this century, their heads stuffed with sentimental mush like *The Idylls of the King*. They feel that every man should play Sir Galahad to their Lily Maid. Even if they turn down his marriage proposal, they expect him to go on being Sir Galahad, yearning hopelessly. And chastely."

But I would not have turned him down, not if he had asked me the day before, or the day before that.

"I suppose you prefer the standards of Paris. Or Venice."

"Right now I wish you'd been raised as a Frenchwoman. I most certainly do."

For perhaps a minute I was silent. Then I said, "Are you going to stay on here?"

"Perhaps. It's a very big house. And I'll take dinner out most evenings. I did before you came here."

"And we keep such different hours that even when we are in the same part of the house, I'm not apt to see you. That is, if you two stay off the balcony."

"Stop that, Sara."

"Why should I?"

"Because you're just hurting yourself. Believe me, I'm sorry about all this."

"Sorry? Or sorry I found out?"

"All right. Sorry you found out. I didn't want you to. In fact, I hoped that after a time—"

"You could have your cake after having eaten it? Well, you can't."

"I see that."

"In fact, you may not have any cake at all. Not in the Belzoni house. Enrico Ponzi is coming home before the ball. In case you have forgotten, Enrico Ponzi is Isabella's husband."

If he also knew that Signore Ponzi planned to stay for only a few days, he didn't say so. In fact, he did not answer.

I said, "I'll go home now. I'd rather you didn't come with me."

"All right. I'll put you in a gondola."

As we moved in silence down the path, I told myself that nothing had changed, really. When I arrived in Venice, I had already renounced Caleb. Now he merely had given me an additional reason for that renunciation.

And in the interval, all that had happened was that I had seen a laughing boy with a dolphin on a bridge—just a little bronze boy with a dolphin. That was how I would try to think of it.

CHAPTER 14

THREE NIGHTS later, I stood in my room in my ball gown, trying to see as much of myself as possible in the dressing table mirror. I did not like what I saw. Compared to dresses of the present mode, with their bustles and peplums, the white gown falling almost straight from its white-ribboned sash just under my bosom seemed scant indeed. My face, paler than usual, would have benefited from some touch of color in my dress. But then, it did not matter how I looked.

I had not seen Caleb at all since I had left him at the boat landing on the Giudecca Channel. He had not appeared in the Belzoni dining room that night, or the night after that, or for tonight's hasty meal at the unwontedly early hour of six o'clock. I guessed that Isabella had not seen him either. The last two nights she had been unusually silent at the dinner table, rousing herself now and then to make some barbed remark to one of her brothers, or to answer, with scarcely concealed boredom, some observation of her husband's.

Enrico Ponzi had arrived two afternoons ago. He was a thin little man, perhaps half a generation older than Isabella, with a bald spot, and with a monocle which he wore, I am certain, not to lend himself distinction, but because the vision in his right eye really was poor. He treated everyone, including his wife, with a kind of absent-minded courtesy. I had the feeling that, soon after the nuptials, he had retreated so deeply into his world of liras, pounds, francs, and dollars, that for long periods of time he forgot he was married.

More than once these past few nights, I had been aware of Isabella's eyes regarding me with speculation in their green depths. I was sure that Caleb had not told her I had discovered their liaison. No matter what he was, he had a certain code, one that would have forbade him to discuss me with Isabella. But instinct had told her that I'd had something to do with his defection.

It wasn't until that hasty supper three hours ago that she had brought the subject up. "It seems that our American friend has deserted us." With a smile that did not reach her eyes, she turned to me. "I wonder if he will even be here for the ball tonight. Do you know, Sara?"

"No."

"I do," Giuseppe said. "He'll be here. I saw him coming out of the costumer's with a box under his arm. I asked him, and he said he's coming as an American colonial. I told him he should come as D'Artagnan. Someone as short as I am looks silly in plumed hat, but Caleb, with his height—"

"Oh, Giuseppe. Stop chattering," Isabella said, but her tone was mild, and her face, tense only moments ago, looked pleased and confident.

When the meal was over, I went up to the Contessa's room, as she had asked me to do. For almost two hours, Maria Rugazzi and I worked to ready her for the ball. We discovered a rent that had to be mended in the gown she wanted to wear—not a masquerade gown because, as she explained to me, the hostess did not mask—but a wine-red velvet dress perhaps twenty years old. We dressed her wig and pinned it firmly to her scant hair. From a velvet box on her dressing room table, a box I had never seen before, I fetched at her order a diamond necklace, badly in need of cleaning, and the slender tiara, also in need of cleaning, which she had worn the night she berated her grandchildren so unmercifully.

At last Maria rang for Emilio. Followed by the housekeeper and me, he carried her to the floor below and installed her in a thronelike chair of green velvet and gilded scrollwork just outside the grand salon. The chair faced the staircase from the Grand Canal entrance to the house, which her guests would begin to ascend at any moment.

She said, after she had waved Emilio away, "I shall stay here only until the last of my guests arrive. Then I shall return to my room. Sara, come there at ten-thirty. You must help me to get out of all this. Maria will be too busy supervising the servants down here."

"At ten-thirty, Aunt Sophia."

I hurried up the stairs, hearing behind me a babble of voices as the first arrivals ascended from the ground floor. It had taken me three-quarters of an hour to bathe in the bathtub of cooling water the maid Louisa had placed in my room, dress, and coax my heavy, quite straight hair into high-piled ringlets, like those in the illustration Isabella had shown me.

The ball was well under way now. Even at this distance, and through my room's closed door, I could hear a spirited polka. By now the Contessa must have returned to her room. Around my neck I clasped the string of false pearls Isabella had loaned me. I picked up my narrow white mask, the only item of my costume purchased by me, and, careful not to disarrange my hair, fastened the mask's elastic band at the back of my head. Then I left the room.

When I reached the hall below, I saw that the Contessa's thronelike chair was empty. I moved to the salon doorway, which tonight was flanked by two impassive, hired-for-the-occasion footmen, and paused there.

The orchestra, on its stand at one end of the room, was momentarily silent. But the babble of a hundred voices confused my ears. And the motley assemblage beneath the huge chandelier confused my gaze. A Columbine moved with her hand resting on the arm of a Barbary pirate. Nearby a Salome tittered at some remark made by a Julius Caesar, while a Marie Antoinette rapped her closed fan against his arm in mock reproof. I saw Pierrots, circus ringmasters, Grecian ladies, and even a red Indian chief.

Gradually my gaze found the few people I knew. Through a rift in the crowd I saw Giuseppe, resplendent in the wig, ice-blue satin coat and knee breeches and high-heeled shoes of a Louis the Fourteenth courtier. He stood against the far wall, alone but not looking lonely. He was surveying the assemblage with obvious pride and delight.

A moment later my eyes found Carlo, standing a few yards away to my right. He listened with an enrapt smile to a girl of about eighteen, thin and blond and pretty in the full-skirted dress and starched lace cap of a Breton lady. But every now and then he looked over her shoulder at a dark-haired Carmen of about thirty, whose left hand, I noticed, wore a wedding ring. Even though she appeared to listen to the Egyptian Pharaoh beside her, her dark eyes, shining through the slits in her red mask, kept meeting Carlo's.

Then, with an almost painful leap of my heart, I saw Caleb. He stood near the bandstand, wearing the cocked hat, blue coat, and knee breeches that had been the everyday dress of his Boston ancestors of more than a century ago. He was talking to Isabella's husband. Perhaps the little banker had thought wearing a costume undignified. More likely, he had forgotten that the occasion was a masquerade. What ever the reason, he was in conventional evening dress, with a red carnation in his buttonhole striking the only frivolous note.

I forced my gaze away from Caleb and Enrico Ponzi. Where was Isabella? In the card room, where champagne and punch were being served? Or hadn't she made her entrance yet? I wondered about her costume. She had laughingly but firmly refused to talk about it to any of us. If she had dressed as Salome, she would be furious, because already there was one Salome here. But, I thought grimly, that still left Jezebel.

"Why, Sara! Why are you standing there?" Footsteps inaudible in the hubbub, Isabella had come up behind me. "Let's join the ball."

I turned around and went rigid with shock and incredulous anger.

Except for two ringlets framing her excitement-flushed face, her red-gold curls were piled high, like those of a lady of Napoleon's court. She wore pearls, undoubtedly real ones, around her slender neck. From the white ribbon sash crossed beneath her full bosom, her slender white gown fell in silken folds.

"Surprise!" She clapped her hands. "I was afraid you'd guess when you saw how much material I'd bought, but I can see from your face that you didn't. Isn't it a lark?"

Encircling my waist with her arm, she drew me into the crowd. I was aware of startled faces, and amused ones, and a few indignant ones, as if their owners guessed the situation. Helpless, wanting to break free of her and bolt from the room, but unwilling to make a scene, I moved ahead, too thin and too pale in my unbecoming gown, beside a woman who was radiantly beautiful in an exact duplicate of that gown.

"Where's Caleb?" she asked.

I did not reply. Why had she done this to me? The answer was obvious. She wanted to show Caleb just how much more desirable she was. But why had she bothered? Surely she had learned that Caleb desired her. And then I realized that probably it was before their liaison had begun that she had suggested—no, insisted—that I allow her to have a costume made for me.

She said, through the opening strains of a waltz, "Oh, there he is, talking to my husband."

Would her husband's presence, I wondered, make her triumph doubly sweet? I won't pull away, I promised myself, and I won't flinch when Caleb looks at me.

The two men had seen us now. "Look!" Isabella cried. "We're not cousins. We're twin sisters. Isn't it a lark?"

After one swift look at her, Caleb fastened his eyes on my

face. His own face was white with anger. He stepped forward, lifted my unresisting hand, and kissed it. "How beautiful you look, Sara."

I felt the hot pressure of tears behind my eyes. He asked, "May I have this waltz?"

Isabella's arm fell away from me. Without looking at her, Caleb encircled my waist with his right arm and clasped my hand with his left. He whirled me into the crowd of dancers.

He said something under his breath, and then asked aloud, "Are you all right, Sara?"

"Yes." But don't be kind to me, I wanted to say. I can't bear it when you're kind.

"You don't want to dance with me, do you?"

"No."

"I can't leave you in the middle of the floor. Come on. I see Giuseppe over there."

I took his arm, and he led me to my cousin. "Giuseppe, would you like to finish this waltz with Sara?"

He said with obvious sincerity, "I would be delighted." As Giuseppe and I moved out onto the floor, I saw Caleb turn and walk toward the card room.

My cousin proved to be an excellent but extremely earnest dancer. With a half-hysterical impulse toward laughter, I saw that as we whirled and dipped and reversed, his face wore the same concentrated look as when he had draped brocade over the shabby salon chairs. It must have been shyness that had kept him off the dance floor until now. Or, I thought, with a flood of fellow-feeling—for I, too, had just been made to feel ridiculous—perhaps he feared that his partners would be laughing at him secretly.

When the music stopped, he said, "I enjoyed that, Sara. You are so light on your feet."

I answered wryly, as we moved off the floor, "It's because I'm thin."

"Don't let anyone make you feel you're too thin." He spoke

with so much force that I knew he must have observed his sister propelling me through the crowd. "You have *distinction,* Sara."

The Barbary pirate approached, was introduced, and asked me to dance. Gratefully aware that I'd be less conspicuous on the dance floor than standing at its edge, I allowed him to whirl me away in a polka. When it was finished, he introduced me to one of the several Pierrots, who asked me to waltz with him. I did, and then, realizing thankfully that it must be ten-thirty, or even a little past, I excused myself and hurried from the salon.

Halfway up the first flight of stairs to the floor above, I halted. Anna sat there on the landing in a nightdress and pink robe.

"Anna! How long have you been here?"

"Only a minute. Please, Cousin Sara! Just a little while longer." The gray-green eyes in the plain little face held not only pleading, but adoration. Such is the gratitude of a child delivered from the horrors of seventeenth-century trade agreements to the delights of Aesop and, only a few days ago, *Alice in Wonderland,* an English edition of which the Contessa had allowed me to order.

"All right." The Belzoni ball came only once a year. "Just a little while." Keeping my face averted from Isabella's portrait, I went up the stairs.

At the Contessa's door I raised my hand to knock, and then lowered it. She was speaking to someone in her harsh voice made even harsher by rage. Because of the thickness of the door and the music rising from below, I could not distinguish the words, but their furious tone was unmistakable. She paused, as if for breath. I heard someone else speak in a voice less loud than hers, but just as angry, only to be overridden by a fresh tirade from the Contessa.

I hesitated for another moment, and then knocked. After a few seconds of silence, I heard the faint squeak of the Contessa's wheelchair. Close on the other side of the door now, she demanded, "Who is it?"

"It's Sara, Aunt Sophia. You told me to come at ten-thirty."

"Never mind what I told you! Go away."

"But when shall I come back to—?"

"I don't want any help. Go!"

"All right, Aunt Sophia."

I turned away, puzzled and concerned. For the first time I realized that I had become fond of my proud, stingy, cruel, and yet sometimes kind old kinswoman. Whatever the cause of her fury, surely it was not worth the strain on her aged heart.

I cast a longing glance toward my room. But no. I would not let people think that I had been driven from the ball. I would not give Isabella the satisfaction of picturing me face down on my bed, crying. I moved toward the stairs.

Anna still sat on the landing, her small face rapturous as she listened to the music. "In fifteen minutes I am going to look up here," I said, "and if I still see you—"

The ravishing smile she gave me was only slightly dimmed by the gap where a tooth had been yesterday. "You won't see me."

In the doorway to the salon I again hesitated. The room was less crowded now. I could not see Caleb nor any member of the Belzoni family. Perhaps they were among the men and women, visible through the archway, who had crowded around the buffet table set up in the card room.

Enrico Ponzi appeared beside me. I had the impression that he had approached, not from somewhere inside the salon, but from the hall. Perhaps he had been down to the courtyard for a breath of fresh air. "May I have the rest of this gavotte, Signorina Randall?"

Isabella's husband was a terrible dancer. As he propelled me this way and that across the floor, his monocle dangling from its string, I saw his lips stir, and knew that he was counting the steps.

When the music stopped, he said, "I must apologize for my dancing. It is not an activity I enjoy."

Had he asked me, then, only because he wanted to make

amends for his wife's behavior? I discarded the idea. From his lack of embarrassment, it was obvious that he had not been aware that Isabella and I wore identical gowns.

"If you do not enjoy dancing, Signore Ponzi, why did you ask me?"

"Because this is a ball, and at a ball one must dance. And I preferred asking you to any of the other ladies."

"Why?"

"Because I have no small talk, and I have observed at dinner that you do not make small talk. If I had told one of the other ladies that she had been my special choice, she might have hit me with her fan and said, 'You naughty man! I have heard what a flatterer you are.' I do not know how to answer ladies who call me a naughty man."

"It would be difficult."

"All I can talk about is finance. To me it is enthralling, but ladies find it dull."

"I think I might not."

His face lit up. "Really? Would you like to hear about a meeting I had with an American and a Frenchman in Paris last week? We could sit at that table out on the balcony. It would be quite proper. We would be fully visible to everyone."

I assented. It would save him the pain of dancing, and others the pain of dancing with him. But the great advantage, of course, was that I could remain in nominal attendance at the ball without being too aware of either Caleb or Isabella.

We sat out there, with the Grand Canal below us, and the brilliantly clad dancers swirling beyond the long, opened windows beside us, while he talked of the Paris meeting. The American had been Andrew Carnegie, and the Frenchman the current Baron Rothschild of the family's Paris branch. I understood little of what had occurred at that meeting in Signore Ponzi's hotel room, beyond the fact that Carnegie was seeking more capital for expansion of his steel plants in America. What fascinated me was the thought of three men making plans that would affect the lives of thousands of workers, and reverberate in financial centers over the world. And of those three, one had been the rough-mannered son of a Scottish weaver, one the grandson of a moneylender in the Frankfort ghetto, and one a little Italian who had an unfaithful wife and no small talk.

At last he said, "Shall I fetch you some champagne, signorina? Or would you prefer wine punch?"

"The punch, please."

He left me. I looked through the balcony doorway at the dancers, and wished I hadn't. Caleb was waltzing with Isabella. From the set expression on his face, I felt that it was only at her invitation that he had taken the floor with her. But that was small comfort. I could tell that she pled with him, a coaxing smile on her lovely, upturned face. How long would he hold out against her? After my conversation with him in that little park, why should he hold out five minutes? And why should I care?

Surely I had stayed here long enough that I could, without loss of face, leave the ball. I would drink wine punch with Enrico Ponzi and then say good night.

He came out onto the balcony, followed by a footman bearing two crystal cups of punch on a tray. The footman held the tray before me, and I took one of the cups. I did not know that the sight of Caleb with Isabella in his arms had set my hand to trembling, not until dark red liquid spilled from the cup onto my lap.

I sprang to my feet and placed the cup on the table. With a pocket handkerchief, Signore Ponzi began to dab at the stain on my skirt.

"It is no use, signore. All I can do is to wash the dress as soon as possible."

"Such a pity! Could you change to something else and come back?"

"I have nothing else suitable. Besides, it must be almost twelve o'clock. Good night, Signore Ponzi. I enjoyed our conversation."

Looking neither right nor left, I moved across the salon and out into the hall. To my relief, because I had forgotten to make sure, I saw that Anna no longer sat on the stairs. I climbed to the floor above, and then hesitated at the Contessa's door.

No sound from within. Perhaps she had summoned someone else to help her to bed. Or perhaps, too angry to sleep, she still sat fully dressed in her wheelchair, brooding.

Who was it, I wondered, who had so enraged her?

I knocked softly. There was no answer.

In my room I stripped off my dress, glad to be rid of its silken touch, and washed it in water from the pitcher. The wine stain faded, but did not disappear. Well, no matter. I would never wear that dress again. And I doubted that Isabella would want her gift back, now that it had served its purpose. I pushed other clothing in the wardrobe to one end of the supporting pole, and hung up the damp gown. Then I finished undressing and went to bed.

Long after the distant music ceased, and even after the musicians and hired-for-the-occasion servants had made their noisy departure from the side entrance below my window, I lay awake, thinking of Caleb. The room's furniture was taking shape in the dawn light before I fell asleep.

A scream, followed by a muffled crash, brought me awake. I sat up in bed, aware of early sunlight in the room and of the alarmed pounding of my heart. Somewhere out in the hall, a voice went on screaming. It sounded like Louisa's. With the confusion of one torn from too-brief slumber, I groped for my slippers, struggled into my robe.

I went out into the hall. At its other end I saw Isabella, in a pink velvet robe, standing rigid before the open doorway of the Contessa's room. Beside her stood Louisa, no longer screaming, her face buried in her hands. A breakfast tray and scattered remnants of broken crockery lay around her feet.

Swiftly, and yet weighted with reluctance, I moved along the hall. Then a door just ahead of me opened, and I saw Anna's small shivering shape and frightened face.

"Don't come out here, Anna. Stay in your room."

Rapid footsteps behind me. I turned and saw Caleb in dark trousers and white shirt. "Stay with the child," he said, "until I find out."

Inside her room, I sat on her small rumpled bed and held her in my arms. Paco, his long chain fastened to a dressing table leg, apparently had been affected by his young mistress's fear, because he did not chatter. He sat still, staring at us with yellow eyes.

"Don't be frightened, Anna."

"What is it?"

"I don't know yet," I said, although of course I did, in a way. Something had happened to the Contessa. "But whatever it is, try not to be frightened."

Someone knocked. I opened the door, saw Caleb, and stepped out into the hall, closing the door behind me. A swift glance to my right showed me that now others crowded around the Contessa's doorway—Giuseppe, and Carlo, and Maria Rugazzi, and the fat cook, Giovanni, and Emilio.

"Is she dead?"

"Yes. You'd better take Anna into your room and stay there."

"Did she—how was she—?"

His gray eyes looked down at me, considering. "You might as well know. She's sitting there in her wheelchair just inside the door. She was stabbed many times. It must have happened beside the fireplace."

Numb with shock, I repeated, "The fireplace?"

"Yes. There's a trail of blood leading from the fireplace to where she finally died. I guess she was trying to get out, so that someone would hear her call."

The last time I stopped at her door, had she been sitting behind it, staring with sightless eyes at the panel upon which I knocked? I managed to move my lips. "Why didn't she—I mean, there's a bellpull beside the fireplace."

"She couldn't have reached it. Someone slashed the lower half of it off, and then stabbed her repeatedly and left her for dead."

In my mind's eye I saw my terrified kinswoman lunge half out of her chair to grasp the bellpull, saw a blade flash as it severed the length of silk cord. Then I saw the knife in the hand of someone faceless, nameless, turn upon the helpless old woman—

"What vitality she must have had," Caleb said, "to wheel herself clear to the door."

And what stubbornness, I thought. What grim stubbornness.

Caleb said, "It would be best for you to tell the child."

"Yes." But I would tell her as little as possible of how her great-grandmother had died.

"Why not take her into your room for a while?" he said.

"All right." I felt grief for my great-aunt and horrified rage at whoever had slain her so brutally. And I felt something else—a dread that I could not put a name to. "I'll get Anna dressed and take her to my room."

CHAPTER 15

About two hours later, someone knocked upon the door of my room.

In the interval, I myself had dressed. Then I had read to Anna, as she lay curled up on my bed, from *Alice in Wonderland*. Little of the story registered upon my mind or, I suppose, upon hers. But it served to distract us somewhat from the sounds outside this room—the bump and scrape of arriving gondolas against the landing stage, and voices of strange men in the hall. Once I heard departing footsteps across the courtyard toward the landing stage—shuffling footsteps, as of men who carried a burden. I saw, from the widened pupils of Anna's eyes, that she knew what the sound meant. She turned her head toward the balcony, where the still-subdued Paco sat chained to the rail, and I laid aside my book, ready to stop her if she tried to go out there and look down.

She did not. But I saw that the book had lost her attention entirely, and so I began to talk of when I had first read *Alice* under an elm tree on the lawn of the house where I was born. I went on to talk of doll tea parties with neighborhood children on that same lawn, and of clamming at the shore and sailing a catboat on Long Island Sound.

"What's a catboat?"

"A small boat, rather like that skiff Emilio sometimes uses when he goes on errands."

"And you could sail it?" For a few minutes at least, she had forgotten Louisa's screams and those shuffling footsteps out in the courtyard. "Oh, Cousin Sara! Will you take me sailing on the Grand Canal?"

"I'm afraid Venetian ladies don't sail skiffs on the Grand Canal."

"But you're an American lady!"

"An American lady in Venice." The disappointment in her face made me add, "But perhaps something can be worked out. Anyway, if I ever do sail the skiff, I'll take you with me."

A knock at the door had come just then. I opened it to see Louisa. Stepping out into the hall, I closed the door behind me. The maid's pretty face still bore traces of the shock she must have felt when she opened the Contessa's door early that morning, but her manner was composed.

"An inspector of police is in the dining room. We must all go down there, at once."

"All of us? Even the child?"

"Not unless it becomes necessary. I heard Maria Rugazzi ask him, and that is what he said."

"Very well." Perhaps it was only because of that other inquest, that coroner's inquest months before in Connecticut, that I felt a heightening of my nameless anxiety.

I went back into my room. "Anna, I must leave you for a while. Do you think you could do your grammar lesson? It would pass the time while I'm gone."

She nodded.

"I'll bring the grammar and your notebook from your room."

"Could you bring Paco's water bowl too? He looks thirsty."

In her room I picked up Paco's new water bowl of red clay, the second one she had molded for him in the last two weeks, and her English grammar, notebook, and pencil box. I returned to my room and settled her to work at my dressing table. Then, still weighted with that strange apprehension, I went to the floor below, crossed the salon, where sunlight revealed shabbiness that must have been invisible to last night's merrymakers, and walked through the card room, now cleared of its buffet table, to the dining room.

As I entered, not only the faces of those seated at the long table turned toward me, but also the faces of the well-trained servants who stood along the wall opposite the baize door. A heightening of the tension in the room told me that all of them, including the stranger at the head of the table, had been waiting for me, the last arrival.

"You are Signorina Randall, the American lady?" The slender man at the head of the table was about fifty, with salt-and-pepper hair and a Vandyke beard as yet untouched by gray. His dark eyes were alert behind rimless glasses.

"Yes."

"I am Leone Pacelli, inspector of police. Please sit down." He nodded toward an empty chair between Carlo and Giuseppe.

I took the vacant chair. Giuseppe, pale and with reddened eyes, gave me a wan smile. As for Carlo, apparently shock had deprived him of his customary gallantry, because he nodded briefly to me and then stared straight ahead. Directly opposite to me sat Enrico Ponzi, with Isabella on his right and Caleb on his left.

"I have called all of you here," Signore Pacelli said, "to try to determine the time of the Contessa's death. And to determine that we must learn who was the last to see her alive."

No one said anything. I stole a look at Isabella, and saw that strain, and perhaps a too-early awakening, had dimmed her beauty somewhat. Morning sunlight, striking through the window, revealed faint lines at the corners of her eyes and bracketing her mouth.

"Well, who was in attendance upon the Contessa last night?" The inspector's gaze, a little impatient, swept the line of servants.

I said, "I was supposed to be." His gaze turned to me. "The servants were of course very busy last night, and so she had asked me to come to her room at ten-thirty. But when I did so, she wouldn't even open the door. She told me to go away and not come back."

"Did she give a reason?"

"No, but there was someone with her. I could not distinguish their words, but they were quarreling."

His gaze sharpened. "Who was the person with her?"

"I don't know."

"Was it a man's voice?"

"I think so, but I couldn't swear to it. The door is very thick, and the music from below was quite loud."

"How long were you outside the Contessa's door?"

"Only seconds, a minute at most. Then I went back to the ball."

He studied me. He held a yellow pencil, balanced teeter-totter fashion, between the first and second fingers of his right hand. He began to tap on the table, first with one end of the pencil and then the other. "Let us see. You are a relative of the Contessa's, are you not?"

"Her grandniece."

"And you came here after an unfortunate happening in America, did you not? An elderly lady in your care came to a violent death. Is that not true?"

Who had told him? Carlo? Isabella? Maria Rugazzi? It could have been anybody. Undoubtedly word of my trouble in America had spread through the household. "There was no question of foul play," I said, aware of Caleb's gaze on my face. Briefly, I explained about the fire. "The coroner's verdict was accidental death."

"Very well. Now to return to the matter in hand. Can anyone verify that you heard the Contessa quarreling with some unknown person? Did you tell anyone what you had heard?"

"No. It was the Contessa's business." I felt rising irritation. "Would you expect me to gossip about it with her guests?"

"I meant no offense. In fact, I am trying to help you. Now

can anyone verify that you returned from the Contessa's room after—how long did you say, a minute?"

My sense of apprehension was growing. "How could anyone have noticed exactly when I returned to the salon? People were dancing, enjoying themselves, not watching to see when I left and when—"

I broke off. Anna! "The Contessa's great-grandchild could tell you. She was on the stairs when I went to the floor above, and she was still there when I came down a few moments later."

"Oh, yes." He glanced at a paper before him. "The little girl, Anna Belzoni. Where is she?"

"In my room, doing her lessons."

His gaze turned to the line of servants. "What is your name?"

"Louisa, Signore Inspector. Louisa Crespi."

"Please go to Signorina Randall's room and bring the little girl back here."

When Louisa had left the room, Caleb spoke. "Signore Pacelli, may I say something?"

"Of a certainty. You are Signore Hayworth, the professor who is here as a paying guest?"

"Yes. I want to point out that there were about a hundred guests here last night, plus ten musicians, and several extra servants."

"I am quite aware of that."

"Then is it reasonable to concentrate your investigation upon Signorina Randall and the rest of us in this room? The house was filled with people last night. What's more, the Contessa might have been killed by someone not even authorized to be here—someone who took advantage of the confusion to gain entry."

"We are aware of that also. But first we are considering those who had the most opportunity to stab the poor lady to death. Does that not seem logical?"

"No!" Giuseppe's voice was shrill. "What reason would any of us have had to—to do that terrible thing?"

"A motive? We have discovered a very strong one."

A stillness settled down. I had the impression that everyone in the room had stiffened, from Maria Rugazzi standing with red-rimmed eyes to the little banker sitting opposite me. A motive, I thought. Then surely the police could have no serious suspicion of me. There was no conceivable reason why I should have wanted the Contessa to die.

"What motive?" Caleb's voice, sounding harsh, broke in on my thoughts.

"I shall tell you that soon. But right now, here is the child. Please come here, Anna."

The small figure moved along the line of servants. When she reached her grandmother, she hesitated. Maria, looking ten years older than when she and I had arrayed her mistress in frayed finery the night before, smiled encouragingly into the upturned face.

Anna moved on to the head of the table. With a friendly ease that told me he probably had raised children of his own, the inspector took her hand in his. "You were on the stairs last night, Anna, listening to the music?"

"Yes."

"And you saw Signorina Randall come out of the ballroom and climb to the floor above?"

She looked at me, and I smiled at her. "Yes," she said.

"Now this is important, Anna. Did much time pass before Signorina Randall came down the stairs?"

"Oh, no. They were playing a polka when she went upstairs. They were still playing it when she came down and told me to go to bed in fifteen minutes, and then went and stood in the doorway of the salon."

"I see. And you didn't hear her go into the Contessa's room, or hear them—talking?"

"I didn't hear anything but the music." She looked bewildered. "Anyway, there wouldn't have been time for them to talk, would there?"

"It seems not. Thank you, Anna."

"Of course, I guess they talked later. Anyway, I saw Cousin Sara coming out of the Contessa's room."

For a moment I felt nothing at all. Then I cried, "Anna!" Her face, startled and a little frightened, turned toward me. "You couldn't have seen me. After the ball started last night, I was never in the Contessa's room."

"But, Cousin Sara! I saw you. I went to my room as I promised you, but I couldn't sleep, so I got out of bed and opened the door a little—"

Signore Pacelli interrupted. "Do you know what time this was, Anna?"

"Yes, eleven. The clock in the Piazza had just struck, and I counted."

I, too, had heard the bronze Moors, high in the Piazza bell tower, strike the hour of eleven. I had been out on the balcony then, listening to Enrico talk of Carnegie and Baron Rothschild. Would he remember the clock striking? Probably not. He had been too engrossed in his story.

I said, "Anna, you must have been dreaming."

Distress in the homely little face now. "I wasn't! I opened the door, so that I could hear the music. Most of the lamps had been put out in the hall, but I could see you come out of the room in your white dress. You walked to the head of the stairs, and you said—"

She broke off, dawning comprehension in her eyes. Signore Pacelli asked, "Said what, Anna?"

"It wasn't Cousin Sara, because she said—"

She repeated a phrase so coarse that even the police inspector reddened.

Carlo let out an explosive laugh. "That couldn't have been Sara! That was Isabella."

The police inspector said, "Well, Signora Ponzi?"

Isabella lifted her chin. The green eyes in her flushed face were defiant. "Yes, I went up to her room last night. I intended to tell you about it."

"Why did you go there?"

"The clasp of my necklace had broken. I took my necklace to my room, and then I went to her room to see if she would loan me her diamond necklace for the rest of the ball."

"She was alive then?"

"Of course! And she was alive when I left her."

"Did she loan you her necklace?"

"No. She might have, if something hadn't made her so angry. She refused me the necklace and ordered me out of her room."

"Was she wearing the necklace?"

"Yes, and her tiara. She was sitting there in her wheelchair, all decked out in diamonds, and looking furious."

"I see. Now as I understand it, the Contessa returned to her room last night as soon as she had greeted the last of her guests. Who took her to her room?"

"I did, Signore Inspector." I looked at Emilio, standing there between Giovanni, the fat cook, and Hortensia, the middle-aged maid. His face was so grave and respectful that one would never have dreamed that he had made advances to his employer's grandniece and threatened to throw his employer's grandson into the canal. "I carried the Contessa to her room and left her in her wheelchair."

"Where she remained, alive and fully dressed," Signore Pacelli said, "until sometime after eleven o'clock, when Signora Ponzi went there to request the loan of her necklace. Or so it would seem."

He paused, and then asked, "Did any of you see or speak to her after the hour of eleven last night? If so, now is the time to say so."

There was no sound in the room.

"Did any of you try to see or speak to her?"

Better not to hold anything back. "After I finally left the ball, I knocked on her door. There was no answer. I assumed she was asleep or just didn't want to see anyone, so I went on to my room. I never dreamed that she might be—"

I broke off. The inspector said, after studying me for a moment, "And this was when?"

"Around midnight. It was five minutes after twelve when I reached my room."

"I see." He smiled down at Anna. "Well, Louisa will take you back to your lessons now."

When Louisa and the child had left the room, he went on, "Now as to motive. Signore Carlo Belzoni already knows this, because I asked him about the Contessa's personal possessions, and he gave me a list of the valuables she kept in her room. She herself had given you that list, I understand."

"Yes," Carlo said. "She gave one copy of the list to her lawyer, and another to me, as the elder grandson."

"A diamond necklace and a diamond tiara were on that list. We found them neither on her body nor in the small safe behind one of the pictures, which Signore Carlo Belzoni pointed out to me."

So there had been a safe behind one of those pictures.

"Another missing object is a gold basin, set with gems. I understand that it is very old and very valuable."

The Constantinople basin. As I had looked at it, there on the Contessa's brocade counterpane, I thought of all the bloody violence—wars and sieges and assassination—that the object must have survived. And now still more blood had been shed for its sake.

"The safe was too small to accommodate the basin," the inspector said, "and yet I understand it was the Contessa's eccentric habit to keep it hidden somewhere in her room."

"I *told* her," Giuseppe said. "I told her it should be kept in a bank vault. But she wouldn't listen."

"Does anyone know where she did keep the basin?"

"I do, Signore Inspector," Maria Rugazzi said. "Years ago she asked me to tack some strips of cloth to the back of her dressing table mirror. Two crossed pieces, tacked at each end, so that they made a kind of sling. You understand, Signore Inspector?"

"Yes. I saw the cloth strips when my men searched her room."

"She wanted to keep it there because Anna liked to play with the basin when she came to the Contessa's room."

"I told her," Giuseppe repeated. "One day when I came to her room I saw that child with the basin in her lap, and I said, 'Grandmother, someday someone will do you great harm because of that thing.' And now—" His voice broke.

Signore Pacelli waited for a tactful moment and then said, "Yes, signore. That was the motive you asked about. The bowl and the jewelry."

Caleb spoke. "That's all the more reason to suspect an outsider, some professional thief who knew there would be more than a hundred people here last night, most of them masked. I don't know what sort of safe the Contessa had, but a professional thief can open almost any safe."

"Anyone at all could have opened this one," the inspector said, "because the combination no longer works. The safe was really no more effective than an unlocked box set into the wall and concealed by a picture."

"Very well, then. The thief could have invested in some sort of costume. He wouldn't have come in by the Grand Canal entrance, where footmen were collecting invitations. But he could have entered the house some other way and slipped up to the Contessa's room."

I pictured a masked man snatching the necklace from the throat of the dying woman, and the tiara from her bewigged head.

"Perhaps you are right, Signore Hayworth. But for the moment—" He turned to Isabella. "Signora, where is the dress you wore last night?"

"In my room, of course."

"Would you object if I sent Louisa to get your dress and

bring it here?" Until he spoke, I had not realized that Louisa had returned, to stand beside Maria Rugazzi.

Isabella asked, "Why do you want to see the dress?"

"Isn't it obvious, signora?"

Of course, I thought. If Isabella had wielded that knife, her white silk dress would have been covered with blood. But surely he could not suspect that Isabella could have murdered her own grandmother. Surely no member of the Contessa's family could have done it, nor any of the servants, all of whom had been in her employ for years. Even Louisa had worked for the Contessa for three years, since she was sixteen, and the others for many times that. Surely Caleb was right. Some professional thief had committed that brutal murder.

Isabella shrugged. "I have no objection to your seeing it."

The inspector looked at me. "And you, Signorina Randall?"

"I?"

"Will you permit the maid to bring your ball gown down from your room?"

My gown. The one I had washed last night, in a vain effort to eradicate the wine stain. The dress that hung, still damp, in my wardrobe. "Well, signorina, will you permit it?"

They were all looking at me. Unable to speak, I nodded.

Louisa left the room. I sat there, heartbeats suffocatingly fast. I must say something before Louisa returned.

"Signore, you will find my dress still damp."

"Damp?"

"I washed it after I left the ball."

"Washed it! A ball gown, and so late at night?"

"I had spilled wine on it. I hoped to wash the stain out before it set, but you can still see it. Signore Ponzi was with me when I spilled the wine."

The little banker spoke for the first time. "That is true, inspector. She spilled wine on her dress. Then she said good night to me, and left the ball."

"How unfortunate," Signore Pacelli said to me, "that you

should have ruined your gown." But there was no commiseration in his eyes, and no friendliness. What was wrong? Surely he could accept Enrico Ponzi's word.

Louisa came back into the room, a white silk dress over each arm. She carried them to the inspector. Getting to his feet, he held up one dress, redraped it over Louisa's arm, and then held up the other. "As you said, Signorina Randall, it is still damp. And one can see the stain. A pity."

Still holding the dress, he looked from Isabella to me and then back again. "I can see why the little girl was confused. To me these dresses appear identical. Did you ladies come to the ball as twins?"

From the corner of my eye, I saw Isabella flush. "It was a joke."

"I see." He laid my dress over the maid's other arm. "Louisa, return Signora Ponzi's dress to her room. Then go down to the side entrance. One of my lieutenants is stationed there. Give him Signorina Randall's dress."

I cried, "Why?"

"Because it is evidence."

"What do you mean, evidence?" Caleb asked angrily. "She explained why she washed the dress. And Signore Ponzi confirmed what she said."

The inspector's voice was cold. "Perhaps Signorina Randall is a more clever young lady than anyone has supposed. Perhaps she spilled wine on her dress, before an impeccable witness, because she knew that soon blood might be splattered on that dress—blood she would have to wash out."

I gave a cry of protest, and Caleb said harshly, "Nonsense!"

"Perhaps. And perhaps we will find no trace of blood on this dress, even if it had been there last night. Bloodstains wash out easily if treated in time—much more easily than wine."

I cried, "You'll find nothing there but the wine stain!"

"In that case, the dress will be negative evidence, but evidence it is. Do as I ask, Louisa."

She left the room. I sat there with my hands clenched in my lap and looked straight at Signore Pacelli. It was hard to do. I had felt blood rush into my face and then drain away, and I knew that I must have given the appearance of a guilty person. But surely no one in the room, with the exception of Signore Pacelli, who did not know me, could think me capable of such a violent, inhuman act.

Caleb said, "You tell us of the Contessa's missing valuables. Why don't you search Signorina Randall's room, if you think she could have killed her great-aunt?"

The inspector smiled faintly. "Her room has been searched. All your rooms have been, while we have been sitting here. Signore Carlo Belzoni gave his permission. I hope you will find nothing too disarranged. My men try to be considerate."

After a moment he went on, "I am sure they have not found the missing items. If they had, someone would have come here to tell me. Nor have they found any clothing that could possibly have been worn by anyone who perpetrated this terrible, bloody deed." The implication of the glance he sent me was clear. They had found no possibly suspect clothing except that damp dress of mine.

Giuseppe's voice was indignant. "So some outsider killed Grandmother, just as Caleb said. You rummaged through our personal things for nothing. I don't mind telling you that I for one resent it."

"I cannot agree with your conclusion, signore," the inspector said. "The absence of the jewelry in the bedrooms does not mean that no one in this house took it. Someone could have found a temporary hiding place somewhere else in this very large house, or outside it. Nor is the absence of bloodstained clothing really significant. Such clothing could have been sunk in any of a score of canals at some time during the night. But I am sorry if the search of your own room has annoyed you.

"You may go now," he went on, "but no one must leave Venice."

Isabella's husband said, "But I must take the train to Bern tomorrow! I have an important conference."

"I regret, Signore Ponzi. None of you must leave Venice. None of you."

CHAPTER 16

At two that afternoon, I was wandering through the maze of narrow streets and little squares behind the Piazza. An hour from now the streets would be thronged. But now most Venetians were observing the siesta, lingering over luncheon in cafés or private houses, or lying asleep behind drawn blinds. Many shop doors were locked, and most of the squares, usually filled with Venetians in gossiping, gesticulating groups, were deserted except for cats drowsing in the heat.

I felt weary and anxious. True, not just Caleb, but the Contessa's grandchildren and Enrico Ponzi had appeared to be indignant upon my behalf. When we had left the dining room, where Signore Pacelli had begun to write in a notebook, and had crossed the card room and salon, we gathered for a few moments in the hall. Giuseppe said, "Imagine that fellow suspecting you, Sara!"

"Or any of us," Isabella said.

Carlo shrugged. "It's a policeman's business to be suspicious."

"Just the same," Enrico Ponzi said, "I think he went too far." But there was reserve in the little banker's eyes as he looked at me. I felt, with helpless indignation, that he wondered if I really had spilled that wine purposely. And perhaps he was not the only one who wondered. They must be asking themselves, too, if I had been completely frank in my letter to the Contessa about the death of my former employer. Perhaps that fire had not been an accident—

Isabella said, "I must rest. I simply must. I'm tired to the bone. Are you coming, Enrico?"

Isabella and her husband climbed the stairs, with her two brothers following closely. None of them looked back at me when they reached the landing. I felt sure they would gather in Isabella's room to talk about the Contessa's death and about me, the foreigner, the stranger, whose only tie to them was the tenuous one of second-cousinship.

Caleb still stood beside me, though. He said, "Don't worry. There's nothing to worry about. Innocent people aren't convicted."

I managed to smile. "What, never?"

He returned the smile. "Well, hardly ever. When they find the jewelry, they'll find the murderer. It's as simple as that. What I wonder about is why the inspector didn't seem suspicious of me. I'm a complete outsider. Why didn't he turn that fishy eye on me?"

"I can think of several reasons. You're a professor, and the Italians have great respect for learning. Did you notice the tone of his voice when he addressed you as Professor Hayworth? What's more, your last employer didn't die in a fire, and you weren't the one the Contessa asked to help her to bed last night, and you didn't have a damp masquerade costume hanging in your wardrobe." My voice broke on the last words.

"Oh, Sara! Listen to me. You need someone now, and I seem to be the only one available. Couldn't we—?"

I shook my head. There was still Isabella, or at least there still had been Isabella. Just because I might be in dire straits, I could not take back all the things I had said in the little park. I had meant those words. To pretend I had not, so as to feel a strong arm around me, would have cheapened me in my own eyes, and cheapened everything I had ever felt for Caleb.

"I'll go to my room now," I said. "Like Isabella, I'm tired to the bone."

On the floor above, I stopped by Anna's room. I found her seated in her armchair—a child-sized one, and yet a little large for her—legs dangling, and with the monkey perched on her shoulder. I had the impression she had been sitting there for some time. How lonely she looked, how lonely she was. In her entire eight years, I had learned, she'd had no playmate except Paco. The only affection she'd had was from her great-grandmother, who now was dead, and from her grandmother, who was too busy, or perhaps too filled with a sense of class differences, too aware that the child carried the Contessa's blood as well as her own, to give Anna more than an occasional brief, almost furtive caress.

Certainly her aunt and uncles felt indifference toward her at best, and irritation at worst. One evening I had come into the dining room just as Carlo was saying something about "Rosa's brat." Rosa, the housemaid who had given birth to Antonio Belzoni's child and then deserted Venice for the Roman streets. Well, I could understand how they might resent the child of their dead brother, whose virtues, whether real or imaginary, were always being held up to them by the Contessa. To make matters worse in the eyes of that handsome trio, their niece was not even pretty.

I said, "We'll have no lessons today, Anna. But I will come to you at the usual hour, and we'll read to each other. Would you like that?"

"Yes."

"Why don't you take your modeling clay out onto the balcony? You could make another figure of Paco."

"All right. Cousin Sara, did I make things bad for you? I really thought I saw you in the hall last night. I guess I was sleepy and—"

"You didn't make things bad. You told the truth, or what you believed was the truth. I'll leave you now, Anna. I must rest."

In my room I exchanged my outer clothing for a light wrapper and lay down. But weary as I was, the sleep I had hoped for did not come.

Around twelve-thirty, Louisa brought me a meal of shirred eggs and sausage, substantial enough to be considered both breakfast and luncheon. This time she did not linger. She placed the tray on the dressing table, shot me a side glance, and left the room.

I lay there, feeling almost literally sick. There had been apparent fear in the girl's dark eyes—fear of the foreign she-devil who had stabbed an old woman to death. For the first time I realized that until my great-aunt's murderer was found, some people in this house would regard me, not just with suspicion, but fear.

It was that intolerable thought which had made me get up from my bed to dress and leave the house and move along back streets through the midday heat and silence.

I must have wandered in a semicircle, because ahead of me, at the end of the street, I could see one of St. Mark's saints standing atop his pinnacle. Turning to my right when I reached the Piazza, I moved along the colonnade that borders the great square. At sight of tables set out before the Café Quadri, I realized I was thirsty.

I sat down at a table. After a while a waiter came to take my order. He brought me a glass of mineral water, accepted payment, and then retreated to the comparative coolness of the arcade.

At this hour the square was emptier than I had ever seen it. A vendor with a rack of postcards slung around his neck stood in the campanile's shadow, waiting for the afternoon crowds to appear. A group of tourists had gathered outside the entrance to St. Mark's. The distant sound of their voices told me they were German. Apparently impervious to the heat, they moved about in their heavy clothes, looking up from different angles at the golden horses who pawed the humid air. Except for the ever-present pigeons, pecking at what was left of their morning grain scattered over the pavement, the square was otherwise deserted.

Footsteps somewhere nearby. I turned my head. A man I had never seen before emerged from the arcade's shadow. He sat down at a table about fifteen feet away, opened a newspaper, and held it before his face.

My heart began to pound. One of Signore Pacelli's men? Had I been followed as I moved aimlessly through narrow streets and deserted *campi*?

I got up and walked away. When I reached the Piazza's western end, I looked back. The man still sat there, reading. Evidently not a policeman. Nevertheless, as I moved away from the Piazza, I resolved to leave Venice the moment Signore Pacelli permitted me to. I could supplement my meager funds by selling my grandmother's ivory fan and a bracelet set with opals left to me by my mother. And I had a few of my father's books—volumes so cherished and so valuable that I had brought them with me. There was a calf-bound set of Vergil, and a copy of Prescott's *Conquest of Mexico,* which the great historian, shortly before his death, had personally autographed to my father. Surely some dealer would pay well for those.

And while I was forced to remain here, I would busy myself by applying again for a teaching post in America. After my father's death, and while I was seeking employment, I had compiled a list of girls' schools in New England and the Atlantic states. I would write to them from Venice, saying that I would be in America soon, and available for a position.

I found the Belzoni house silent, its wide halls deserted. When I reached my room, I placed my valise on the bed, opened it, and took from a side pocket the important papers I had placed there—my parents' marriage certificate, the bill of sale for my father's house, and my teacher's certificate. I had expected to find the list of girls' schools, but it was not there.

Then I remembered. Thinking I might never need that list again, and certainly not while I was in Venice, I had placed the list in one of the books I had packed in the bottom of my trunk. Because this room had no place to keep such bulky volumes, they had remained in the trunk when Emilio took it away.

Where had he taken it? The attic, almost certainly.

Leaving my room, I climbed the stairs. In the archway to the narrow fourth-floor hall, I hesitated, looking down its dim length. Then I told myself not to be foolish. Even if someone, that afternoon more than three weeks before, had waited in one of those rooms for my departure—waited in such angry fear that I had sensed his emotion—no harm had come to me because of it. Harm had come only to poor Aunt Sophia. And the man who killed her, almost certainly, had been some thieving stranger. I hurried along the hall and up the narrow stairs.

In the attic I saw that no one had restored those articles dislodged by Paco's scrambling progress along the shelf. The leather chest, bronze vase, and jardinière filled with broken fragments still stood lined up against the wall. About fifteen feet farther along the wall stood my trunk.

I raised the lid. There they were, about a dozen of the many books which had lined my father's study. I found the list in the Prescott history. Thrusting the paper down the front of my dress, I descended from the attic and walked back between the rows of closed doors.

I had almost reached the end of the hall when a man entered through the archway. After an alarmed instant, I saw he was Giuseppe. We both halted, regarding each other with the faint embarrassment of people meeting in a place where it is unusual, if not actually forbidden, for them to be. In his hand he carried a rectangle of heavy drawing paper.

I said, "Hello, Giuseppe. I've been up to the attic. I left a list of addresses in my trunk up there."

"Oh." He paused, and then went on rapidly, "I'm going to leave this sketch in Emilio's room. The poor fellow is too shy to pose for me, so I've had to draw it as best I could." He held it out to me.

It was a recognizable charcoal sketch of Emilio in his gondola, the long oar poised for the downward stroke which would send his craft forward. The sketch showed that Giuseppe had mastered certain technical problems of drawing. But it lacked the sense of life which Anna infused into her untutored little sculptures of pigeons and cats.

"If I gave it to him in person," Giuseppe said, "he'd be so embarrassed that he'd pretend to be annoyed, and so I'll just leave it for him. Not, of course, that I expect it to appeal to him."

"I'm sure it will," I said mendaciously. Even if, by some miracle, the genius of a Leonardo had guided Giuseppe's hand as he made that sketch, the surly gondolier would have scorned it.

"Well," I said, "I have correspondence to attend to. I'll see you at dinner."

On my way down to my room, I suddenly wondered if it had been Giuseppe's footsteps that had approached the attic steps that day and then halted, Giuseppe who had waited behind an almost closed door for me to return to the lower part of the house. I was still almost a stranger to him then. As far as he knew, I might have been the sort who would mention at dinner that I had seen him in the servants' quarters, and thus hold him up to the ridicule of his brother and sister.

Then I dismissed the whole matter. I had far more immediate concerns than Giuseppe. I spent the rest of the day writing the first three of my letters and reading to Anna.

Dinner that night was a strained affair. There was none of the usual banter between Isabella and her brothers. Nor did anyone mention the Contessa, except for Carlo's brief reference to the funeral, which would be held the day after tomorrow on San Michele Island. I felt that if Caleb had not drawn Enrico Ponzi into a discussion of Renaissance banking methods, the meal might have passed in almost complete silence.

What was more, I felt, just as I had after that session with the police inspector, that the Belzoni brothers and Isabella and her husband were eager to be rid of my presence. As soon as dinner was over, I exchanged good nights with them. No one suggested that I linger. Even Caleb, perhaps knowing how uncomfortable the meal had been for me, just gave me a warm smile and said, "Good night, Sara."

When I reached my room, I wrote one more letter. Then, overwhelmed by fatigue, I went to bed and fell asleep almost immediately.

In the morning I tried not to mind when Louisa, after bringing my tray, hastily withdrew. Soon I would be away from the distrust in her once-friendly face, and away from this house and Venice.

I wrote more letters and then, so early that I knew there was little chance of meeting anyone, went down to the luncheon buffet in the dining room. Afterwards I again escaped the house to wander through the midday heat past closed shops and shuttered windows. Once I paused in a *campo* to look at a church which I had seen many times, but which never failed to bring me incredulous dismay. (With a pang, I recalled an especially happy afternoon when Caleb, standing beside me here, had described how this particular church had provoked Ruskin to fury.) The church, designed and paid for by a rich seventeenth-century general, displayed not one religious symbol on its façade. Instead there was a statue of the general in full uniform, flanked by statues of Honor, Virtue, Fame, and Wisdom.

How typical of Venice, I thought, this city where so much was not what it seemed to be. How typical that a man could build a monument to his own monstrous vanity and call it a church.

On my way back to the Belzoni house, I noted the location of a still-closed bookshop and of a jeweler's, where I might be able to sell my father's books and the bracelet and ivory fan. I also stopped in a mercer's shop, which was just reopening its door, and bought a spool of brown thread. The hem of my bombazine traveling costume was about to come loose. Better to attend to such small matters, so that I would be ready to leave Venice as soon as I was granted permission.

When I reached the house, I gave Anna her lessons. Then I went to my room and took the brown bombazine from the wardrobe and laid it on the bed. Standing on tiptoe, I took my sewing box down from the wardrobe shelf.

It seemed much heavier than I remembered. Puzzled, I placed it on the dressing table, opened its lid, and lifted out the tray which held scissors and packets of needles. Then I removed the rest of the box's contents—balls of cream-colored wool, knitting needles, and several layers of ribbons in varying lengths and colors.

I found myself looking down at a muslin-wrapped bundle which had not been in that box when I packed it in my trunk in Connecticut.

Heartbeats faint and rapid with a premonition of what I would find, hands shaking, I turned back the folds of the bundle. The diamond necklace and tiara, both so badly in need of cleaning, gleamed in the late afternoon light striking through the balcony windows.

CHAPTER 17

"WHEN THEY find the diamonds, they will find the murderer." Was it Caleb who had said that, I wondered, hearing the pounding of my heart, or the police inspector?

Until this moment, I had believed in Caleb's theory. Some professional thief, seizing the opportunity offered by the masquerade ball, had slipped into the house and killed and robbed the Contessa.

But now I knew it was no outsider who had wielded that knife. Some member of this household had stabbed her, snatched the diamonds from her dying body, and then placed them here, so that I, already suspect in the eyes of the police, would appear guilty beyond any doubt.

Someone knocked.

For a moment I stood frozen. Then I seized the flannel-wrapped bundle and thrust it beneath the counterpane of my bed.

Again someone knocked. I said, "Who is it?" and then realized, too late, that perhaps I should have stepped out onto the balcony and dropped the jewelry into the canal before I answered.

"It's Caleb, Sara."

Weak with relief, I crossed the room and opened the door. He said, "I was wondering if— Sara! What is it?"

I raised a shaking finger to my lips. He came into the room, closing the door behind him. I turned back the counterpane and unfolded the small bundle.

He stared at the necklace and tiara for a moment. Then, without a word, he picked up the bundle and thrust it into his coat pocket.

I said, "Caleb, I didn't—"

"You don't have to tell me that."

"What are you going to do?"

"Mail the jewelry to the police. Anonymously."

"Wouldn't it be better to throw it into the canal?"

"You'd probably be seen. Someone in a gondola or at a window in this house or the one opposite—"

"After dark, then!" Never mind, I thought wildly, that the diamonds were not mine to so dispose of. Right now my freedom, even my life, was at stake.

"You haven't got until after dark. The police will be here soon. I'm sure of it." He started toward the door and then turned back. "The Constantinople basin. Is it here?"

I said, feeling the blood drain from my face, "I don't know."

He, too, was pale. "We'd better find out. And fast."

In our haste we did not take the time to move quietly. I searched the bureau drawers and my valise and the wardrobe. Caleb turned back the mattress on the bed, and moved the dressing table and bureau out from the wall. The basin seemed to be no place in the room.

I cried, "My trunk! Maybe it's been put in my trunk."

"Where?"

"The attic. It's a big leather trunk with my initials. It isn't locked."

"Give me the trunk key."

"I told you! It isn't locked."

"It should be. Even if the basin isn't in it now, it may be put there later if you don't keep that trunk locked."

I took the key from the top bureau drawer and gave it to him. He said, "Try to get this room back together again."

I tried, panting, while he was gone. I swept the mattress back so that it again lay flat, drew the bed coverings into place, and shoved the washstand back against the wall. I was trying to move the heavy bureau when I heard Caleb's knock and his low voice.

He came into the room, closing the door behind him. "It's not there," he said, and handed me the trunk key. He shoved the bureau back into place. Then he said, "Last night's dinner was so awful that I was going to suggest taking you out tonight. But it's better that neither of us do anything unusual. Wash your face, Sara. It's dusty. And for God's sake, be careful of what you say. The diamonds won't be here. You must act as if they were never here."

He left me. I washed my white, dust-streaked face, smoothed my hair. Hurriedly I restored the contents of the bureau drawers to neatness. Then I sat down to wait, hands clenched in my lap.

I did not have to wait long. About twenty minutes after Caleb's departure, there was a knock at the door. I said in a voice that was almost as calm as I had hoped it would be, "Who is it?"

"The inspector of police, signorina."

I opened the door. Signore Pacelli stood flanked by two uniformed policemen. "Yes?" I said.

"Will you permit us to search your room?"

While I waited, I had decided it would be best not to seem too readily compliant. "But, signore! You said all the rooms had already been searched."

"There's a reason for my request. It would be easier if you were co-operative, Signorina Randall."

I said after a moment, "Very well," and opened the door wide.

As Signore Pacelli had said, his men were considerate. They caused far less havoc than Caleb and I had in our wild search for the basin. Methodically they went through the wardrobe, valise, and bureau drawers, restoring each possible hiding place to order before they moved on to the next. They turned back the bedclothes and mattress, replaced them, and looked behind the draperies. When they had moved out the dressing table and bureau and then shoved them back into place, Signore Pacelli said, "We are sorry to have disturbed you, signorina."

"Don't you think you owe me an explanation?"

"We received an anonymous note through the mail."

My heart beat faster. Perhaps the handwriting– "May I see it?"

After a moment's hesitation, he took out a black leather notecase. From it he extracted a folded sheet of white paper, unfolded it, and handed it to me.

With mingled disappointment and anger, I read the note. Words had been scissored from some printed matter and then pasted to the paper to form one sentence: "Contessa Belzoni jewelry in American woman's room."

Signore Pacelli said, "We are sure the words were cut from yesterday's newspaper. As you can see, the words 'Contessa Belzoni' and 'American' are in the large type used for headlines, the others in small type. Yesterday's paper carried news of the Contessa's death, with her name in the headline, of course, and two unrelated stories in which the word 'American' appeared in the headline."

I handed the note back to him. "And you have no idea who–"

"How could we? The note came through the mail, with only the word 'police,' also cut from a newspaper, pasted to the envelope. Some stupid clerk at the post office must have been confused by the incomplete address, and laid the letter aside temporarily, because it did not reach us in the afternoon delivery. Someone at the post office, finally realizing that it might be important, sent it over to us by a messenger half an hour ago."

And so, if it had not been for that blessedly stupid postal clerk, the police would have been here, searching my room, while I was out wandering the streets or in Anna's room giving her her lessons. I felt sweat spring out on my upper lip, and hoped the inspector did not see it.

He asked, "Did you read the newspaper account of the Contessa's death?"

"No."

"It listed the members of the Contessa's household, including you. You were referred to as the Contessa's American-born grandniece. And so someone with a twisted sense of humor, or perhaps some grudge against Americans, cut words from the newspaper to form this note. It is not unusual for the police to have such jokes played upon them."

But in this instance not played upon the police. Upon me, and by someone who was not joking.

"I apologize for our intrusion. And I bid you good evening, Signorina Randall."

He and the two uniformed men started toward the door. I said, "Inspector." He turned.

I tried to make my voice light. "What if you had found the Contessa's jewelry in this room?"

"Surely you realize the answer to that. I would have arrested you immediately."

"For the Contessa's murder?"

"Yes."

"Even though you found no blood on that ball gown? You see, I am sure you did not."

"Even so you would have been arrested. After all, the dress had been washed. Incidentally, it will be returned to you shortly."

"What is the penalty for murder in Italy, inspector?"

"What it is in most countries. Death." He, too, made his voice light. "And so let us congratulate ourselves that there was no necessity for such an arrest."

"Am I free to leave Venice?"

"I am sorry, but no. No one in this house can leave Venice until we have made an arrest for the Contessa's murder."

"Then may I move to a hotel?"

His manner, so courteous a moment before, subtly changed. "Why should you desire to do that?"

What reason could I give? That until a few minutes before his arrival, the jewelry had indeed been in this room? I said, "It isn't pleasant to stay in a house where someone has been murdered."

"I realize that. Few things concerning a murder are pleasant. But all of you will make the task of the police easier by remaining where you are. In fact, I must insist. Again, my apologies for this intrusion. Good day, signorina."

When they had gone, I locked and bolted the door. Then I went out onto the balcony and stood there in the red-gold light of near sunset, gripping the rail. Through my fear, a cold, determined rage was rising. Someone in this house had not only brutally murdered my aunt, but tried to destroy me.

Turning, I stood with my back to the rail and looked up at the spot from which that head had fallen. I was no longer sure that its fall had been an accident.

I had a sense of a pattern, of lines connecting seemingly unrelated events—that lurker on the servants' floor the day after my arrival in Venice, and the head hurtling down, and the footsteps hurrying after me along the fog-choked streets, and the Contessa's death. Perhaps there were other lines, to happenings that had seemed of no consequence at the time. A kind of web, with someone sitting spiderlike at its center.

Well, I thought grimly, since I had to stay here, it would not be as a caught, helpless fly. I would find the spider.

But I would be careful. Whenever I was not in my room, its door would be locked, even though I realized that there were probably duplicates in the house of that heavy old key. When I was in my room, its door would be both locked and bolted. And I would try to see to it that I never found myself alone with any adult member of this household except Caleb.

CHAPTER 18

Soon after we sat down to dinner that night, I said clearly, "Did any of you know that the police visited me late this afternoon?"

From the wary but unsurprised faces that turned toward me, I realized that they all knew it. Carlo said, "Yes, the inspector spoke to me before going to your room."

Caleb was watching me with alarm. I sent him a reassuring glance and then said to Carlo, "Did he tell you his reason for the visit?"

Carlo's handsome face was impassive. "No."

"He had reason to think that the Contessa's stolen property was in my room. Someone had sent the police an anonymous note to that effect. His men searched, but of course they found nothing."

There was complete silence for several seconds. Then Carlo turned to his sister and asked coldly, "Another of your jokes, Isabella?"

Her green eyes grew more brilliant. "No! And I might ask the same question of you, although more than likely it was Giuseppe. It's the sort of sneaky thing he might do."

Giuseppe laid down his fork so hard that it rang against the plate. "I resent that, Isabella!"

Enrico Ponzi said irritably, "It was probably some crazy eccentric. Perhaps tomorrow the police will get a note accusing me."

To judge from his expression, the thought filled him with almost uncontrollable choler. Then, after a moment, he turned to Caleb. "I looked up that point you mentioned about the Medici last night. According to the usury laws of that time—"

While the banker went on, I covertly studied his face and that of his wife and brothers-in-law. They all looked irritated and sullen. But for one of them, was sullenness a mask for a stronger emotion? Was one of them wondering, with frustrated fury, what had become of those objects hidden in my sewing box? I could not tell.

At last Carlo turned to me and said, "Do you plan to attend Grandmother's funeral tomorrow?"

"Of course. She was my great-aunt."

"Very well. The funeral procession will form at the side entrance to the house. I have hired extra gondolas to carry the family and servants. There will be many more gondolas, of course."

"Is Anna to attend?"

"Certainly. Everyone would be shocked if she did not."

It was on the tip of my tongue to say that a funeral was no place for a child, but I thought better of it. If all the servants were going, she would be left alone in the house. And if one of them stayed—well, how could I be sure that she had not been left with the person who had wielded that knife?

Isabella had been listening from across the table. Now she leaned toward me. "And you will attend the reading of the will day after tomorrow, of course. It's to be held in the grand salon at ten in the morning."

"I don't understand. Why should I be there?"

Her green eyes sparkled. "Grandmother's lawyer tells us she left a sum to be divided among the servants. I asked him if that includes you, even though you'd been in her service less than a month, and he said yes."

Score one for Isabella. But was it rage that had made her so eager to score—rage over that jewelry the police had not found in my sewing box?

I said as serenely as I could, "I will be glad of anything Aunt Sophia may have left me." For the first time I wondered how large an estate my seemingly impoverished kinswoman had left. One thing was certain. Giuseppe would use at least part of his share to restore those salon side chairs.

When the meal ended, I said, "Caleb, will you please see me to my room?"

"Of course. Good night, everyone."

Aware of the surprise in the men's faces and the surprise and anger in Isabella's, I, too, said good night and walked with Caleb from the room.

As we moved across the salon to the hall, he said, "You gave me quite a turn when you spoke of the inspector's visit. I wanted to shout, 'Sara! Don't stir up the animals!'"

"I could tell you felt that way. But they must have known that the police found nothing to incriminate me. Otherwise I'd have been arrested. And if one of those four others at the table tonight hid that jewelry in my room, he—or she—already knew that somehow I had found it before the police got here."

He nodded. "And that somehow you'd gotten rid of it. Yes, I realized that a moment after you'd asked them the question. Incidentally, the jewelry is already in the mail."

Neither his face nor his voice had registered any protest at the idea that Isabella might be guilty. Then perhaps, inexplicable as it seemed to me, she really had meant nothing to him. Could he have been right that day in the little park? When it came to the relationship between the sexes, was the education of women in this supposedly enlightened nineteenth century—well, unrealistic?

As we neared my room, he said, "Lock your door tonight. And don't let anyone in until I call for you in the morning. We'll go down to the landing stage together."

"No one? Not even Louisa with the breakfast tray?"

"Tell her to leave it in the hall."

It seemed absurd to be afraid of Louisa, when her fear of me was so obvious. Perhaps it was a little too obvious. I considered Louisa for a moment. She was indiscreet, vain, and flighty. No doubt it had occurred to her that jewelry was wasted upon an old woman who spent all her time in a wheelchair or in bed. I could imagine Louisa, on one of those rare occasions when the Contessa was absent from her room, slipping in to try on the diamonds, clasping the necklace around her pretty neck, and taking off her white cap to place the tiara on her glossy dark curls.

Yes, Louisa was the sort to covet jewelry. She was also the sort who, if tempted into thievery, might go into a panic afterward and try to rid herself of what she had stolen. And as a servant, she had easy access to both the Contessa's room and mine. Still . . .

"I don't think it was Louisa." Reaching into my pocket, I took out the heavy key and handed it to him. "She might be capable of theft, but not of murder."

He turned the key in the lock. "Just the same, have her leave the tray in the hall. Tell her you don't feel well, and want to stay in bed longer. Good night, Sara."

Early the next afternoon, I stood at the Contessa's graveside among the marble monuments and tall cypress trees on the cemetery island of San Michele.

It was not until almost eleven that morning—a gray morning, but oppressively hot—that the Contessa's funeral procession finally had set out across the lagoon. The wide-hulled hearse, its glass and elaborately carved dark wood gleaming dully in the gray light, was in the lead. The Belzoni gondola, carrying Carlo and Giuseppe, and rowed by Emilio, followed directly behind it. Isabella and her husband were in the next gondola, a hired one. So was Caleb. As he and Anna and I had walked down to the courtyard that morning, he had said that he intended to ride with us. But on the landing stage Isabella had said, "You will come with Enrico and me, Caleb."

Her eyes had sparkled so dangerously that even if Caleb or I had cared to we could not have protested, not without making a scene.

Anna and I rode in the next gondola, followed by two more hired gondolas, which carried the servants. Still farther back, strung out for perhaps a mile across the lagoon, were private gondolas bearing dark-clad members of the oldest and most noble families in Venice. Most of them, in masquerade finery, had greeted the Contessa as she sat outside the grand salon only a few nights before. I had a sudden vision of how the procession would look to some balloonist—a long line of graceful black vessels, each casting its reflection and that of its muscular oarsman onto water that gleamed like gray satin.

I looked at Anna, sitting so quietly beside me in her thin black cloak and in the black bonnet Maria Rugazzi had hastily made for her. What thoughts were going on behind that homely little face? Was she realizing that now the only one of her own blood who loved her was her grandmother? I wondered if she ever thought about her dead father or her mother. She had never mentioned either of them to me. But such seeming lack of interest in her origins, a lack unnatural in a child, made me believe that she did think of them often.

In the church on the island, Anna had sat beside me during the long funeral service. Then, with the rest of the Contessa's family and with her servants, we moved through the church's side door to the Belzoni plot, with its crosses and angels of Carrara marble.

As I stood at the graveside listening to the priest intone the final words, I was aware of the solemn faces around me. On one of those faces, that look of composed grief was a mask, hiding God alone knew what frightened, or triumphant, or still-vengeful thoughts. But which face? Carlo's puffily handsome one? Isabella's, so beautiful behind its thin mourning veil? Her husband's, in which impatience seemed at war with his sense of propriety? Or was it the face of Giuseppe, who stood next to me? No, I thought, as I heard his strangled sob. Even though the Contessa had seemed more scornful of him than of her other grandchildren, Giuseppe was the only one who had taken pride in her imperious ways, and felt real affection for her.

One of the servants, then? From under half-lowered lids I looked at the line of them on the other side of the grave. Maria Rugazzi, still appearing ten years older than when she and I had dressed the Contessa for the ball. Always I'd had the impression that she felt the Contessa justified in sending Rosa away—erring Rosa, who had proved just how depraved she was by using the money the Contessa gave her, not to open a *campo* stall or to support herself thriftily until she found other employment, but to rent a Rome apartment and buy the flashy finery of a cocotte. Nevertheless, Maria must have still loved her daughter, however much she agreed with the Contessa's judgment that Rosa be banished. For eight years, while she devotedly served the Contessa, her heart often must have been heavy with grief. And perhaps three nights ago something—perhaps some remark of the Contessa's—had caused that grief to flare into violence.

I looked at Emilio, standing there in frayed mourning livery. I knew the gondolier to be sly, cynical, and bold. What was more, on the island of Santa Theodosia he had hinted to me that he might be rich soon. Perhaps he was capable of killing an old woman for her jewelry. But once he had it, would he have parted from it so quickly, placing it in my room for the police to find? I did not think so, not unless some overwhelming reason had arisen.

Next to him stood Louisa, pretty and pert-looking despite her cheap black dress and the black shawl framing her face. Beside her was that unwilling spinster, Hortensia, her middle-aged face plainer than ever now that she wore an unbecoming black hat rather than the white cap I was used to seeing. The appearance of the cook, who stood at one end of the row, seemed the most altered. Sometimes, when Giovanni left his kitchen for the comparative coolness of the courtyard, I had caught a glimpse of him from my balcony. Always he had been in a white uniform, topped by his mushroom-shaped cap. Now his bulging waistline strained the buttons of a shabby black coat. His jowled face was somber, but perhaps it was his altered prospects he mourned, rather than the death of an employer who had paid him so poorly. Carlo Belzoni might not keep him on. And if not, he might have trouble finding another family willing to hire, at any wage, a cook who had served a prison term for violent assault.

The first clod of earth thudded down on the coffin which held all that was mortal of the great-aunt I had known so briefly. Taking Anna's cold little hand in mine, I moved with the others to where the gondolas waited at the boat landing, black against the gray water.

CHAPTER 19

It rained during the night. Aroused by the drumming on the balcony, I lay awake for a while, picturing the cypresses of San Michele Island bending in the windy dark, and the blurred white forms of the marble angels, and the fresh mound of earth from which the water must be running in rivulets.

When I again awoke, it was to a sunny but quite cool morning, a brisk, businesslike morning, suitable for the matter at hand, the reading of the will.

I had begun to dress when Louisa knocked at the door. "Your breakfast, signorina."

"I'm not quite ready to open the door. Please leave the tray in the hall."

"Again?"

The surprise touched with indignation in her voice made me feel foolish. But I had promised Caleb. "Yes, please."

Apparently her bewildered annoyance at my behavior had outweighed her fear of me, at least for the moment, because she said pertly, "I find you very strange, signorina." Then I heard her walk away.

I had eaten breakfast, set the tray outside in the hall, and finished dressing when Caleb came to the door. He said, surveying my white blouse and blue poplin skirt, "That's a very serious-minded costume. You seem to be prepared for the reading of the will."

"I am, except for a point of protocol that puzzles me."

"What's that?"

"Do I sit with the family, as the Contessa's grandniece? Or do I stand with the servants, as a sharer in their legacy?"

He grinned. "Be sure to tell me which way it turns out. I'm off to the city archives. Yesterday Ponzi and I had an argument about whether Venetian bankers helped to finance Garibaldi, and I want to clear it up. But I'll be back around three. Suppose you set Anna to her lessons. And then suppose you and I take a *burchiello* over to the mainland and have dinner at a restaurant there."

I had been eager to ride in one of those luxurious closed barges furnished with armchairs and lamp tables like a private railroad car in America. But I was still resolved to part with Caleb as well as with Venice. Grateful as I had been the last few days for his protective strength, I still felt we were both too stubborn, too set in our separate views of right and wrong, to make a good marriage. I did not want to risk being tempted again from that decision. The pain with which I'd paid for two days of happiness the week before had been too sharp for me to chance becoming that vulnerable again.

I said, "Thank you, Caleb, but I'd rather not."

His stubborn eyes looked down into mine. "Just the same, I'll ask you again at three."

He locked my door for me, and I pocketed the key. We walked together as far as the salon entrance. There he left me and went on toward the side courtyard.

Evidently it was not yet ten, because only one man, a stranger, sat at a narrow but richly carved table which had been placed in one corner of the vast room. Before him on the table lay a vellum-covered document which I assumed to be the will. As I approached, he got to his feet, a pleasant-looking man of forty-odd, with blue eyes behind glasses, and graying blond hair. He said, "You must be Signorina Randall, the American lady. I'm Leonardo Corsi, the late Contessa's lawyer." And then he solved the problem of my status by pulling back a chair for me.

After I sat down, I looked up at the ceiling, where enormous swans drew a chariot across a blue heaven, in which both clouds and angels floated. Giuseppe had told me that the two handsome passengers in the chariot were a seventeenth-century Belzoni and his bride. The fresco had been painted to celebrate the wedding feast held more than two centuries ago in this room. I had wondered why the Belzonis had chosen this rather than some more intimate room in which to gather this morning. Now I realized that only the grand salon, where once an emperor had been entertained, was worthy to be the setting of this most important occasion, the official transfer of Belzoni wealth—or what remained of it—from dead hands to living ones.

The lawyer said, "Have you read the newspaper this morning?"

"No."

"The police have recovered the poor Contessa's necklace and tiara. Whatever subhuman creature killed her must have become frightened, because he mailed the jewelry to the police. Anonymously, of course."

Bless you, Caleb. I said, "I'm glad."

"Of course, the Constantinople basin is still missing. It's worth far more than any number of necklaces."

Yes, still missing. And it was up to me to make sure that it was not found in my trunk or taped to the back of my bureau.

Footsteps crossing the salon now. Isabella and her husband and her brothers came in and took places at the table. The gratification in their faces, particularly Isabella's, made me think that they knew the jewelry had been recovered. Then the servants came in and stood against the wall's faded damask. I saw Louisa give me a curious side glance before she folded her hands and looked decorously straight ahead.

Signore Corsi exchanged greetings with the new arrivals at the table. I noticed a coldness in the lawyer's manner, and wondered at it briefly. Perhaps the Contessa had confided to him her opinion of her grandchildren, or perhaps he had formed his own opinion from what he had heard from other sources. He said in an official tone, "Are we ready to begin?"

Carlo said, "One moment, Signore Corsi. Should Anna Belzoni be here?"

"No, there is no need for the child's presence."

As Carlo asked his question, there had been tension in the faces at the table. Now it was gone. But before I could speculate about it, the lawyer opened the vellum-bound document and began to read.

The will, dated almost one year before, dealt with the servants' legacy first, naming a sum to be divided among "all those in my employ at the time of my death." The division was to be made solely on length of service. Those in her employ less than a month would receive a certain percentage of the total sum, those with a month to a year's service a larger percentage, and so on. I did some mental arithmetic and concluded that with my share I could buy, if so disposed, two fairly substantial dinners at a second-rate café or two light luncheons at the Quadri.

The next paragraphs dealt with legacies to family members. Carlo, "who makes his living on the stage, and who has so far failed to marry," was left a sum which I judged to be equivalent roughly to what he received for one season at the Metropolitan Opera House. Giuseppe, "who has disappointed me in more ways than I choose to set forth," received a somewhat smaller sum. Isabella, "whose husband, whatever his other failings, is at least capable of supporting her," was awarded a still smaller sum. Enrico Ponzi received nothing.

"The remainder of my property, both real and personal, including all cash moneys, the house where I now dwell, and all my jewelry, paintings, and *objets d'art,* including most especially the Constantinople basin passed on to me by my ancestors, I bequeath to my great-granddaughter, Anna Belzoni, natural daughter of my beloved grandson, Antonio Belzoni.

"I hereby appoint my lawyer, Leonardo Corsi, as Anna Belzoni's guardian and trustee.

"This testament signed on the twelfth day of—"

The lawyer did not finish reading that sentence, because by then Carlo was on his feet and leaning across the table. He brought his fist down beside the vellum-bound document. "I will not stand for this! I'll have the will broken."

"And I'll help you," Isabella's husband snapped.

"She must have lost her senses," Giuseppe said. "The way it starts, 'being of sound mind,' that couldn't have been true."

Signore Corsi said, "The Contessa had herself examined by an alienist the day after this will was drawn up. He attested in writing to her sanity. And she had other legal advice than mine in the drawing up of this will. No, I'm afraid it cannot be broken."

Isabella, sitting on his right, her face flushed, muttered something I did not catch. The lawyer turned to her and said, "The child's mother does not figure in this, Signora Ponzi. Anna is the Contessa's natural great-granddaughter, legally acknowledged as such shortly after her birth, and therefore legally entitled to receive whatever share of the estate the Contessa chose to bequeath her."

"You deliberately misled us!" Carlo shouted. "You said there was no need to have the child present. And all the time you knew—"

The lawyer's cold smile told me that, no matter how gentle his appearance, he was capable of malice. "There was no need. As Anna Belzoni's guardian, I can adequately defend her interest at this table, and in court, too, if that becomes necessary."

"She must have been out of her mind," Giuseppe mourned.

Unnoticed by anyone, I rose from my chair and walked out of the room.

CHAPTER 20

On the floor above, I unlocked the door of my room, relocked it after I was inside, and sat down to exchange my slippers for walking shoes. Let the battle rage below. I had concerns of my own to attend to.

With the key to my trunk in my pocket, I climbed to the fourth floor. I was sure that today I would encounter no one. The servants were still in the salon, standing fascinated, and would remain so until some distracted member of the Belzoni family noticed their continued presence and dismissed them. Nevertheless, I moved hurriedly along the dim aisle between the rows of closed doors.

In the attic, I removed the Prescott history and the set of Vergil from my trunk, and relocked it. With the books in my arms, I hurried from that dusty place back to my room. There I placed the books, my grandmother's fan, and the opal bracelet in my valise. After locking the door behind me, I set off for the third time in the last few days through the narrow streets.

About half an hour later, I returned, carrying the now-empty valise. A wind had sprung up, sweeping loose papers along the streets and roughening the waters of the canals so that wavelets washed over entryway steps. I had sold the fan and bracelet for less than I had hoped to. The Vergil and Prescott, though, had brought me considerably more than I had expected from a book-dealer who had looked at the great historian's signature with almost reverential delight. I now not only had passage money, but enough to keep me for a few days in New York until I found some sort of summer employment. In the fall, surely, I would be able to join the staff of some girls' school.

The salon, I saw as I passed it, was now deserted. I went up to my room. According to my clock, it was not quite twelve. Isabella and her brothers seldom appeared at the dining room buffet before one o'clock. Besides, today they might go to a restaurant, not just for food, but a council of war out of earshot of the servants. I put my valise in the wardrobe, my reticule with its precious banknotes in the top bureau drawer, and then, after locking my door, started down the hall.

The Contessa's door stood open. When I reached it, I saw that Maria Rugazzi was in there. She stood on a stepladder, taking down the last of the draperies. The others lay on the floor in a heap of dark red velvet and frayed white satin lining. She turned her head to smile at me, and then descended the ladder, the heavy draperies in her arms.

I walked into the room. She said, "These draperies have long needed freshening." She shook one out, releasing a cloud of dust, and then began to fold it.

For the first time it struck me that this woman, going about her accustomed tasks, was the grandmother of a child who now owned this vast marble pile and everything in it. I said, "You must have been very pleased and surprised about Anna."

"Not surprised, signorina. The Contessa told me about the will almost a year ago, right after she made it. She told no one else, only me."

"That lawyer seems nice."

"He is a fine gentleman. I was so happy when the Contessa told me she had named Signore Corsi as Anna's guardian. He and his wife have two daughters near Anna's age. She has always been so lonely, my little Anna."

"You mean she is to live with her guardian and his wife?"

"Yes, until she is of age. She will be much happier with them."

"But what about you?"

"I will be able to see her often. But I will remain here. I have worked all my life. I want to keep on working."

Yes, she should keep on working, I thought, looking at her erect figure, her strong hands busy with the draperies. It was hard to imagine her sitting in unaccustomed finery, those work-roughened hands folded in her lap.

I said, "But the Contessa's grandchildren. They won't be here, will they?"

"If they choose to stay. After you left the salon this morning, Signore Corsi read something the Contessa had added to the will. A co–col–"

"Codicil?"

"Yes. It permits Signorina Isabella and her husband and brothers to live in this house if they choose. I suppose Signore Carlo will pay the servants' wages, though, or Signore Ponzi."

I could imagine the Belzonis' reaction when they had been told they would be "permitted" to live in this house. For the first time since the reading of the will, I began to feel a little sorry for them, even Isabella. Well, it was no affair of mine. As soon as the inspector allowed me to, I would leave Venice.

But I would not be allowed to until the police learned who had murdered the Contessa. Murdered her for what? Her jewelry? When one considered how quickly her killer had parted with the diamonds, hiding them in my room for the police to find, it seemed likely that theft had been only a cloak for the real motive. What was it, then? The estate that he or she had expected to inherit? I thought of those flushed, raging faces in the salon that morning, and no longer felt so sorry for the Belzonis.

Maria said, "Next I will do the pictures." The stack of folded draperies in her arms, she looked about the room. Light flooding in, now that the draperies were down, showed the furnishings to be even shabbier than I had realized. "All those picture frames need washing."

The pictures. I walked over to a painting which from the first had especially interested me. It was *Midsummer Picnic,* by a follower of Longhi, and it had the sinister elegance which the master and some of his imitators brought to even the most innocent subjects. You felt that the liquid being poured into a cup by the richly gowned hostess at the picnic table might be poisoned, and that the basket of fruit proffered to a guest by the bewigged and velvet-clad host might contain an asp. As for the pine tree beneath which the table stood, its heavily needled branches were so dark and set so closely together that a madman might crouch hidden up there, ready to drop with a howl into the company's midst.

From the doorway Maria said, "Good-by, signorina. It is time for lunch in the servants' hall."

I turned my head and smiled an acknowledgment. It was not until she had walked away that I realized, feeling amused, that I had spent at least five minutes alone with her—I, who had resolved not to be alone with any one member of this household if I could help it.

I looked at a Maggiotto portrait of a young girl playing a lute. Then I moved across the room to look at the ancient chart of the Venetian lagoon hung beside the ornate headboard of the Contessa's bed, which had so stirred my imagination that first morning after my arrival in this house. My eye moved from the island of Venice to San Michele, where the Contessa lay buried, then to the glass-manufacturing island of Murano, and then on toward Santa Theodosia, where Emilio had caught his eels and I had stood in the long-deserted little chapel looking at the Byzantine Madonna . . .

I caught my breath. Imposed upon the tiny oval that represented Santa Theodosia was a bloody fingerprint. It was very faint, as if the dying woman had barely managed to touch the parchment before falling back into her wheelchair. While the heavy draperies were still up, shutting out most of the light, that stain must have been almost invisible.

As I looked at it, my heart began to pound. In my mind's eye I saw the mortally wounded woman propel herself across the room. Not to try to open the door or cry for help loudly enough to be heard through the heavy panel. She must have known she had not the strength for that. And yet she had tried to leave a message—a message about the island of Santa Theodosia and her murderer.

I still stared at the chart, but I really was not seeing it. I was beginning to see the pattern now, a pattern that linked the sound of footsteps along the fourth-floor hall, and the marks of Emilio's muddy boots on the broken tiles of a long-abandoned chapel, and this faint red stain on the parchment map.

I checked my racing thoughts. Begin at the beginning, I ordered myself. Begin with the footsteps.

The afternoon of my first day in this house, someone—almost certainly Emilio, I realized now—had started toward the attic to investigate the noise Paco and I were making up there. Then he had changed his mind. Why? What was it that had made him decide instead to wait behind a barely opened door, probably his own, until he had seen me leave? Just the sound of my voice? Or some other sound?

I visualized that area of dusty attic floor as it had looked that day, littered with objects Paco had dislodged from the shelf. An overturned leather chest, spilling its envelopes onto the floor. Fragments of china vases and small statuary, now smashed beyond repair, a bronze vase which had reverberated like a gong as it struck . . .

Perhaps that bronze clangor had alarmed him. But why should it?

And then I remembered that envelope which had landed well apart from the others. Thinking that nevertheless it belonged with them, I had placed it in the chest. But now, forcing myself to return in memory to that moment when I knelt on the attic floor, hurriedly scooping up envelopes, I recalled that when I stretched out my arm to gather in the stray one, I had reached, not toward the chest, but the vase. And I had taken fleeting notice of something else about it. What was it, what was it? I strained to visualize my hand picking that envelope up from the floor. Yes, I remembered now. In tall handwriting, it had been addressed like the others to the Contessa. But its ink, unlike that of the others, had been unfaded.

What if Emilio had placed that letter in the vase, considering the attic a far safer hiding place than his own room? And it would be, I thought, with mounting excitement. No member of the Belzoni family was apt to visit that dim, cobwebby place, let alone look in a damaged vase set high on a shelf. As for the consignment of luggage or hopelessly broken-down furniture to the attic, Emilio would be the one to take it there. One couldn't imagine the fat cook or a woman servant carrying a bureau or armchair up those steep stairs. And as the unbroken layer of dust on the floor that day had testified, not even Emilio had been up there for a long, long time.

Why he should have hidden the letter, or why it was so important to him, I could not know. But I felt sure that it was important, so much so that it had led, in one way or another, to the brutal death of a helpless old woman.

Again I checked my thoughts and forced them to return to Emilio, waiting in such angry alarm that I sensed it, behind the almost closed door of a fourth-floor room. Why had he been so frightened? The answer seemed obvious. While I had packed envelopes, including the one that had landed near the vase, into the leather chest, he had pictured me opening that letter and reading it.

And so that night he had leaned out of the window of an unused fourth-floor room and, with a crowbar or some similar instrument, sent that giant head hurtling down toward the marble bench where I sat. And two days later, as I moved through streets choked with fog . . .

Again I tried to impose order upon my rushing thoughts. Go back, I told myself, to the morning after the head fell. I considered his odd behavior that morning, his reluctance to take me to Santa Theodosia Island, and then, after we arrived there, his bold advances to me. Now I realized that his behavior could have been prompted by more than amorousness or a malicious impulse to annoy. Probably he had wanted me to do exactly what I did do—walk away toward the other end of the island, leaving him free to do more than catch eels.

I pictured those muddy boot prints on the chapel floor, prints that had led over to the Byzantine mosaic and then back to the doorway. When I told my great-aunt about them, she had replied scornfully that if Emilio had walked over to the mosaic, it had not been for religious or esthetic reasons. He had been "up to no good." Perhaps he had been contemplating prying the mosaic loose and selling the pieces to some dealer for reassemblage.

She had been wrong, I was sure, about his plans for the mosaic. But she had been right, I was equally sure, about his having been up to no good.

I stood there in my great-aunt's silent room, my whole body tense now. If that envelope with the Contessa's name and address written in that distinctive hand was still up there in the leather chest where I had placed it, then the whole pattern I had been tracing would dissolve into thin air. But if it was not in the chest, then almost surely it lay, wrapped in some sort of waterproof material, beneath one of the time-loosened tiles on that chapel floor.

I turned toward the doorway, and then halted. Might I encounter Emilio up there in the hot dimness of the top floor? My stomach knotted at the thought. But there was almost no chance of meeting him. The meal in the servants' dining room would be a prolonged one today. They would discuss with relish the uproar after the reading of the will, and figure out how much each was to receive of the servants' legacy, and speculate as to who would pay their wages from now on. Yes, I could almost certainly slip up there and back without anyone knowing.

And if I did meet someone? I would say that Paco had gotten loose, and I was searching for him.

I saw no one as I hurried to the marble stairs, up to the top floor hall, and along it to the attic stairs. The little leather chest was sitting just as it had been, against the wall. I opened it and, with hands made awkward by haste, began to lift out envelopes, perhaps a dozen at a time, and go through them. They were all business correspondence, to judge by the return addresses—a Neapolitan wine seller, Florentine leather craftsmen, and Venetian tradesmen of every sort. Some had been postmarked as many as forty years ago, and the ink on all of them had faded to brown.

The letter I sought, the one addressed in still-black ink and a tall hand, was not there. With a sense of triumph, I rose from my knees. Then, as an afterthought, I lifted the vase and looked into its greenish depths. It was empty.

Only one thing remained for me to do up here. I had to make sure that the room where someone had waited behind an almost closed door was Emilio's.

Descending the attic stairs as quietly as I could, I went to the third door on the right. I listened. No sound from inside. After a moment I tried the knob. It turned easily under my hand, and I went into a musty-smelling room, closing the door behind me.

Its shades had been drawn against the hot sunlight, leaving the room dim. Nevertheless, I saw immediately that it was Emilio's. A striped jersey lay on a chair back, and his wide-brimmed gondolier's hat, which he sometimes wore and sometimes did not, lay on the seat. On the straw matting carpet rested Giuseppe's charcoal sketch, ripped in two.

Now that I was here, should I make a hasty search through that rickety bureau and through that battered wardrobe standing, with one door open, at the foot of the rumpled bed? After all, there was a chance the letter was here. But the chance was a small one. Besides, I would have had little taste for such a search, even if it had not been so dangerous. Better to get away unobserved while I still could.

I turned back toward the door and then halted, the pulse in my throat leaping painfully. Footsteps were approaching along the hall—masculine footsteps that were heavy, but not heavy enough to be the cook's. A nightmarish picture rose before me, one I had suppressed until now lest it destroy my courage—Emilio, wielding a knife upon a struggling, pleading old woman in a wheelchair.

I tried to gather my panic-scattered thoughts. What was it I had planned to do if— Oh, yes! "Paco!" I cried, and knew with despair that I had failed to keep my voice from shaking. "Where are you, Paco?"

The door opened. Emilio stood there, shoulders filling the doorway. At first his heavily handsome face was empty of everything except surprise. Then his eyes narrowed.

I said, "The monkey got loose." My voice still shook. Would anyone hear me if I screamed, away up here at the top of the house? "I thought he might have come in here."

"In here?" Although he had taken a step toward me, he was still blocking the door. "How could the monkey get in here? I left the door closed." His voice was a trifle thick. Evidently the servants had celebrated their legacy with a few extra bottles of wine at the midday meal.

"No," I said, "it was open. That was why I thought he might have darted in here."

"I almost always close it." But I could see he was beginning to doubt that he had today. "Did you look in the wardrobe?"

"Yes." I restrained an impulse to try to slip past him. "I looked there."

"Did you look under the bed?" He was beginning to smile in the same way he had when he held my upper arms, there on the Santa Theodosia boat landing.

"Yes."

"In the bed?" He looked at the bed's disordered covers. "That monkey's pretty small. It could be under the blankets."

My voice was at last under control. I said coldly, "I'm sure Paco is not in the bed."

"I'm sorry the bed's messed up. But then, I don't often entertain ladies in my room."

Now he had given me ample excuse for a swift departure. I said, "Please stand aside."

He did not move. "Leaving so soon? I came up here to take a nap. All that yammering at lunch tired me out." He stretched, arching his muscular chest toward me. "But I wouldn't mind talking to you for a while."

"Allow me to leave this room!"

Voices on the back stairs leading up from below, Louisa's voice, and Hortensia's. Grinning, he moved aside, and I walked past him.

I had taken only a few steps down the hall when he called softly, "I hope you find it."

I whirled around. Had he realized all along that I was looking for the letter? "What do you mean?"

"Why, the monkey! I hope you find it."

CHAPTER 21

Inside my room, I relocked my door and then sank trembling onto the chair. Should I go to the police now and tell them that on the island of Santa Theodosia they might find a letter linking Emilio to the Contessa's death?

No, I must not tell them that. The letter might not be there. In that case, all I would have accomplished would be to re-focus their attention upon myself. Once that happened, Signore Pacelli would review our conversation after his men had made their vain search of my room. Why, he might ask himself, had I seemed so reluctant to remain in the Belzoni house? Could it be that I had some guilty knowledge of the jewelry, after all? Could I have mailed it to the police, or given it to someone to mail for me?

No, for the time being I had better stay away from the police.

I glanced at the clock. One-fifteen. Should I just sit here until Caleb returned at three o'clock? Perhaps. But that would be almost two hours from now. And during that time, what would Emilio be doing?

Like Louisa, I considered the gondolier a stupid man, the dangerously stupid sort who believes himself so clever that he can commit even a heinous crime and not get caught. But surely even a stupid man would wonder why I had whirled around in the hall to ask, "What do you mean?"

I could picture him up there on that messy bed, hands crossed behind his head, as he wondered why I, who had told him only minutes before about the missing monkey, apparently had forgotten the object of my search. And after not too long he might guess what I really had been looking for. If so, what would he do then? Row over to Santa Theodosia? Most certainly, if the letter was there. But first he might come looking for me.

Were Carlo and Giuseppe somewhere in the house, or had they, as I had surmised they might, gone out somewhere for luncheon, leaving the fat—and probably drunken—Giovanni as the only man in the house besides Emilio? Even so, I did not think Emilio would dare to break into my room. But he might, if he became convinced I was dangerous to him. As I stared at the bolt on my door—a bolt that might come loose at one thrust of a brawny shoulder—I felt perspiration roll down my sides under my clothing.

I had to get that letter before Emilio did, and put it in the hands of the police. Once he was arrested, I would be safe. But not until then.

How, though, could I get to Santa Theodosia? The public landing stage would be deserted both of gondoliers and customers at this time of day. And I had neither the strength nor the skill required to row the Belzoni gondola.

The skiff! It would be easy for me to row that light craft along the side canal. Once its sail caught the breeze that today must be stirring the wide waters of the Grand Canal, it would move swiftly, perhaps more swiftly than even a powerful man could row a gondola. Out on the lagoon, the wind would be even stronger.

I left the room and, pausing only long enough to relock my door, hurried down to the side courtyard. I realized that perhaps even now Emilio was rushing down the servants' stairs, intent upon reaching the gondola—or my room. All I could do, I thought, as I hurried through the breeze-stirred heat of the courtyard, was to pray that he still lay upon his frowzy bed, puzzling over my behavior or, better yet, sleeping off the wine he had drunk. In that case I would have a good chance of getting away unobserved by him or by anyone who might tell him I had taken the skiff.

I was fumbling with the skiff's mooring line when an outraged voice called, "Cousin Sara!"

Heart leaping, I looked up. Anna stood on the balcony of her room, small face filled with indignation. "You promised me that if you ever–"

The finger I raised to my lips silenced her. After a moment she turned and disappeared inside her room. With despair I realized that she was coming down for an explanation, and that I would have to wait for her. If I did not warn her not to, she almost certainly would run to someone–her grandmother, perhaps, or Louisa–with the news that I had taken the skiff. And then Emilio might hear of it in time to prevent me from reaching the island, or, if I had reached it, from leaving it alive.

Anna was running across the courtyard now. I moved swiftly to meet her. Crouching so that my face was on a level with hers, I said softly, urgently, "I can't take you with me."

Her answer was accusing, but mercifully low in tone. "You promised!"

"Anna, listen to me. I'm going to trust you, because I must. I'm going over to Santa Theodosia Island. I'm certain there's proof there that Emilio killed your great-grandmother. If he learns where I have gone, he will follow me, and I will be in great danger. Can you understand that?"

The small face was white now. She nodded.

I threw a swift glance toward that low archway, through which Emilio might appear at any moment. Then I said, "You must tell no one where I've gone, or even that you saw me leave. That's the one way to make sure that Emilio doesn't find out. Do you understand?"

"Yes," she whispered.

"Then go back into the house and let me get away from here."

She scurried back across the courtyard. I moved to the landing stage. I got into the skiff, lifted the light oars from its floor boards, and fitted them into the locks.

CHAPTER 22

Once I was out on the Grand Canal, I took in the oars and lifted the small sail. The hot breeze, impeded now and then by a bend in the canal, was intermittent, but even so I moved faster than I could have by rowing.

Except for an occasional barge, the canal was empty of traffic at this hour. But the astonishment on the few faces I did see—faces of men on the barges, and of a maidservant looking out a ground-floor window—told me that my surmise had been correct. Venetian ladies did not sail skiffs on the Grand Canal or, perhaps, anywhere else. Once a man on a barge called out something after I had passed. Probably it was fortunate that the breeze died just then, so that his words were drowned out by the rattling of the sail.

Out on the lagoon the fitful breeze became a gusty wind. Every now and then I looked back to see if a gondola, oared by a familiar broad-shouldered figure, was moving swiftly after me. Otherwise I tried not to speculate about what Emilio might be doing, or whether I would find the letter or what it might contain. The sail and the tiller needed all my attention if I was to keep my craft from heeling too far in a sudden gust, and keep its bow pointed toward the low green island that was Santa Theodosia.

When I was only a few yards offshore, I lowered the sail and fitted the oars into the locks. For a moment I considered rowing around the island until I found the sort of brackish inlet where Emilio must have collected his eels. If I left the skiff there, it might be invisible to anyone approaching across the lagoon. Then, if Emilio arrived, I might be able to hide myself in one of the ruined buildings until he left.

But no. I was afraid of those poisonous snakes, even though the Contessa had said they kept to the tall grass at the island's other end. Besides, hiding the skiff would take time, and my best hope of safety lay in a speedy search and withdrawal. I maneuvered the boat to the low, rotting dock, secured it to a weathered mooring pole, and stepped ashore.

Wind bent the grass on either side of the path. As I passed the monastery, I heard wind keening through the broken roof and along the aisle between the doorless cells. Otherwise there was only a hot silence. I moved swiftly to the chapel. In its doorway I did not pause, but hurried across the broken tiles to where the Byzantine Madonna, with the unsmiling Child in her arms, looked out from her niche over a long-vanished altar.

Directly below the mosaic was a tile which, although neither broken nor tilted, seemed to have raised itself a fraction of an inch from those bordering it. Kneeling, I lifted the tile out and laid it aside.

I stayed motionless for a moment, unable to believe that I had found so easily the object I sought. A folded piece of heavy black cloth, of the sort used to cover gondola cabins, lay on the octagon of damp earth I had revealed. With unsteady fingers I picked up the cloth and unfolded it. Inside was the envelope, addressed in tall script to the Contessa, which many days ago I had placed in the leather chest in the Belzoni attic. As I picked it up, I saw that it had been mailed from Padua almost nine years before.

Aware of my racing pulses, I got to my feet, reached into the envelope, and took out a folded sheet of paper, written on both sides. I looked at the salutation, "Dearest Grand-mother," and then turned the page over to read the signature,

"Antonio." Antonio, the beloved grandson who had died of a sudden hemorrhage in a Padua sanitarium months before his illegitimate daughter was born.

Turning the page over, I read:

Dearest Grandmother,

I can see why you had to write your last letter. And yet it brought me pain. How could you have believed for an instant that the girl was telling the truth?

Dearest, I make no pretense of chastity. In a soldier, that would seem absurd. But even if Venice were not full of complaisant young women, which it is, I would not have seduced Rosa. Even if she had attracted me, which she did not, I would not have seduced a servant in your household. I have far too much respect and love for you.

Perhaps the girl expected that because my illness has taken this turn for the worse, you would just accept her word without seeking confirmation from me. Or perhaps she hoped that even if you did write to me, I would be too ill to read your letter, let alone reply to it. In any case, the reason for her lie is plain. She hopes you will give her money before you turn her out of your house.

If you do give her money, I will not object. Now that my first anger upon reading your letter has cooled, I bear only a small grudge against her. And after all, her situation is unfortunate. She will need money to live on until her child is born, and she can seek employment.

But enough of Rosa.

My health is much improved. In fact, I am writing this as I sit on a bench in the sanitarium garden. Soon I will be able to return to Venice and convalesce pleasantly at Ca' Belzoni.

I see the doctor coming, so I must close.

With deepest affection, your grandson,

Antonio.

Despite the optimism of that last paragraph, the hand in which it was written had lost its firmness, and its lines slanted toward the bottom of the page, as if composing even a short letter had drained the writer's strength.

I raised my eyes and stared, completely confused, at the broken mosaic on the wall. If this letter told the truth—and for me, at least, it rang with truth—then the child the Contessa had cherished as her great-granddaughter had not one drop of Belzoni blood.

But Antonio must have been lying in this letter, because later on, perhaps made remorseful by an awareness of approaching death, he had confessed in writing that he was the father of Rosa's unborn child.

But wait! Had he actually written such a confession?

My mind went back to the morning after my arrival in Venice. My Great-Aunt Sophia lying in the ornate bed, her voice brooding as she said, "He was dying by then, and too weak to hold a pen. Not that his letter said so. Being Antonio, he wanted to spare me grief as long as possible. He said it was because he had injured his hand that he was dictating the letter to another patient."

Another patient! Suddenly I was sure—triumphantly sure—that the letter the Contessa had received had not been dictated to a patient in a sanitarium. It had been dictated to one of the public letter writers who offer their services to the illiterate and semi-literate in Italian cities.

And the one who dictated it? My thoughts rushed triumphantly on. Not the Contessa's dying grandson, but a gondolier. A gondolier in league with a servant girl who wanted enough money to go to Rome after her child's birth and set herself up in the profession to which she aspired.

Surely it was Rosa, and not the thick-witted Emilio, who had thought of the scheme. I could imagine how, on Rosa's instructions, he had gone to nearby Padua and approached a letter writer in some public square. "I want to dictate a letter for a friend of mine, a fellow named Antonio, who's sick in a sanitarium. He's dying, in fact, but he doesn't want his grandmother to know that, so just have him say in the letter that he's dictating it to another patient, because he's hurt his hand. Anyway, he has this thing on his conscience about a girl named Rosa . . ."

When the letter was finished, he must have said, "Don't bother to address the envelope. I'll take the letter to his grandmother." Because certainly Rosa would have realized that if the public letter writer knew the Belzoni family was involved, he would guess that he was being made a part of some sort of swindle. No, Emilio must have taken the envelope to someone else to be addressed.

If that was the case, probably my great-aunt had given little thought to the fact that the envelope's handwriting differed from that of the letter. Probably she had concluded that the "fellow patient" of her beloved Antonio, perhaps because of the approach of a doctor, had handed the blank envelope to still another patient to address.

And the genuine letter from Antonio, the one I held in my not-quite-steady hand? Well, Emilio distributed the mail in the Belzoni household. I had seen him more than once climbing the stairs toward the Contessa's room and Isabella's, a silver tray of envelopes in his hand. Intercepting a letter would have been a simple matter for him.

As to why he had kept this letter hidden all these years, first in the bronze vase and then here on the island, I did not know or at the moment care. The important thing was that I had won my race. With this letter, and the bloody fingerprint on the chart, and my account of Emilio's boot tracks on the chapel floor the day he must have hidden the letter here, surely the police would have enough evidence to arrest him on suspicion of murder. Let them puzzle out the whys and wherefores. I would be safe from him, and free, after not too long a time, to leave Venice.

A shadow fell on the broken mosaic—the shadow of someone's head and shoulders.

With a strangled cry, I whirled around and then went weak with relief. It was Maria who stood there in the doorway silhouetted against the mid-afternoon sunlight.

I leaned, shaking, against the rough wall. "Maria! How did you get here?"

"I rowed Emilio's gondola."

I felt admiration that she had done it, this strong but aging woman, and thankfulness that she had. Even if Emilio finally learned of my departure and guessed where I had gone, he would have to take time to hire or borrow some sort of craft to get here himself.

I said, "How did you know I was here? I told Anna to tell no one."

She smiled. "The child did not think that 'no one' meant her grandmother."

"No, I suppose not."

Her smile had died. "She came to me almost at once and told me where you had gone. She said you believed you could find proof that Emilio killed the Contessa."

I answered her unspoken question. "I did find it."

She was looking at the letter in my hand. "Is that paper proof?"

"Yes, at least part of it," I said, feeling suddenly wretched. Until now I had been too absorbed by the triumph of my discovery to think what it would mean to Anna and Anna's grandmother.

"May I see it?"

"There isn't time. We must get back. If Emilio comes here, maybe not even the two of us—"

"He won't come here. After the child came to me, I went to his room. He was asleep. He drank a lot of wine today, celebrating the legacy. All of them did except Hortensia and me. I woke him up and told him that if he'd take the Contessa's paintings down to the laundry and wash the frames, I would unlock the family bin in the wine cellar and give him a bottle of brandy.

"You see," she added, "the laundry windows don't face the courtyard. I wanted to be sure he did not see me take his gondola."

So while I sailed the skiff, there had been no need to fear, each time I looked back, that I would see Emilio, tall body lunging forward as he sent his slender craft in pursuit. Emilio must have been down in the laundry by then, soapsuds matting the dark hair on his arms. "That was very wise of you, Maria."

"Thank you, signorina." She held out her hand. "Now may I see that paper?"

I looked at the lined face. Perhaps, I thought with cowardly hope, she could not read. And then I remembered the Contessa saying that she could read, although haltingly. In fact, a few times before I joined the Belzoni household, the Contessa had set her to reading aloud.

Feeling as if it were a cup of hemlock, I extended the letter.

I watched her bowed head as she read it, moving her lips. What must they make her feel, those words which revealed that her beloved Anna was not the daughter of the Contessa's grandson, and thus perhaps not entitled to possess, upon reaching her majority, that marble *palazzo* and its neglected but still valuable contents?

She handed the page back to me. I restored it to its envelope and put it in the pocket of my skirt. She said, "So that is what was in the letter."

Confused, I looked at her. Her voice had been dull and sad, but there had been no shock in it, or even surprise. "You—you almost sound as if you knew about this letter."

"I did, signorina. Oh, not nine years ago, when Emilio stole it. I learned about it three weeks ago, the day after you arrived here. Emilio came to me then. He was frightened. Under that bluster of his, signorina, he is a cowardly man, afraid of anything he cannot bully with his fists. And he is a stupid man."

I nodded.

"He told me about the letter he had kept hidden in the attic all these years, and that he thought you might have read it. He was afraid you would tell all the Belzoni family about it."

"I didn't read it. I put it back where I thought it belonged. I don't read other people's mail. Not usually."

"I told him you were probably that sort of person. But he was still afraid of you."

"And so that night," I said with mingled anger and remembered terror, "he pried that head loose and sent it hurtling down on me."

"Yes, he could have done that. The mortar holding those heads is very old. Often I told the Contessa that she should have them taken down, but always she said she could not afford to."

And the next day, I thought, he had watched me walk away toward the viper-infested high grass. But no snake had bitten me, nor had he been able to overtake me, the following afternoon, as I hurried through fog-shrouded streets. And as the days passed and the Belzoni family gave no sign that I had told them of the letter, he must have decided that I had not read it, after all.

I said awkwardly, "Maria, I can see why you would not want to. But once you knew of the letter, didn't you have an impulse to tell the Contessa about it?"

"No, signorina. The Contessa was happy in the belief that Anna was her Antonio's child. And Anna—oh, signorina, it was not because I wanted her to inherit wealth that I kept silent. It was because I wanted her to live, someday, with the guardian the Contessa had named, that nice Signore Corsi, and his wife, and his two little girls. And also I did not want Anna to know that she had neither a father or mother to be proud of."

"Do you know who—?"

"Emilio told me three weeks ago that some bargeman had been Anna's father, some married man. I don't know what Rosa would say." Her mouth twisted. "I have neither seen my daughter nor heard from her since she left Venice."

After a moment I asked, "Do you know what Emilio planned to do with Antonio's letter?"

"What he finally did do. He planned to go to the Contessa and tell her about it. He would tell her that if she did not give him a lot of money, he would let all Venice know that the child she had thought was her great-granddaughter was not that at all. And everyone would laugh at her."

"But, Maria! He stole that letter almost nine years ago. If he planned to blackmail the Contessa, why did he wait so long?"

"I asked him about that three weeks ago, signorina. He said that all those years he had been afraid his scheme would not work. He was afraid the Contessa would just dismiss him or have him arrested. He had no certainty that the Contessa really valued Anna, not just as Signore Antonio's daughter, but for the child's own sake. Then, a year ago, he felt he could be certain."

"Because she changed her will? But he could not have known about that. You said you were the only one the Contessa told."

"Sly and thieving people, signorina, have ways of finding out things. Because her lawyer keeps no private gondola, the Contessa always sent Emilio to fetch him and then take him home. On his way home that day a year ago, after the Contessa changed her will, he asked Emilio to stop at his tailor shop. Perhaps he did not know that Emilio can read. Anyway, he left a leather case with his papers in it in the gondola. Emilio rowed around to a side canal out of sight. He opened the case and read the will."

I could imagine the gondolier, standing there in his craft, hurriedly turning the pages until he saw Anna's name. I could imagine his triumph as he read what seemed to him proof of how much the Contessa loved the child, and of how eager she would be to protect Anna as well as herself from the humiliation he could bring upon them. If it had occurred to him that the will might be the result of long-accumulated fury at her grandchildren, rather than overwhelming love for Anna, he must have brushed the thought aside.

I said, "He was taking a chance. If Signore Corsi had come out of the tailor shop before Emilio could get back—"

"But he did not." She shrugged. "And if he had, Emilio would just have apologized and said he had gone on some small errand of his own."

"And you say Emilio did demand money of the Contessa?"

She nodded. "The night of the ball."

I could see why he had waited for that night. It would be the best night, from his point of view. All Venice, or at least all of it that mattered to the Contessa, had been gathered in the grand salon below. He had counted upon her imagining how her guests would look—some shocked, some pitying, some gleeful—if they learned that the great-granddaughter she had prized so highly for eight years was in reality not only the daughter of a housemaid-turned-harlot, but of a canal bargeman.

"And so it was Emilio I heard quarreling with the Contessa?"

Again she nodded.

I considered that quarrel. At some point surely the Contessa had demanded that her grandson's letter be placed in her hand. The gondolier must have answered, "Not until I get the money. And don't think you can find it and destroy it. It's not even in this house any longer." Perhaps, with frustrated anger confusing his not-too-strong wits, he had added, "Nobody will find it, because nobody but me goes there."

But even if he had not added something like that, the Contessa could have guessed. I had told her of Emilio's muddy footprints on the floor of this chapel. She knew that Santa Theodosia–thanks to the snakes that kept picnickers away, and thanks to Emilio's fists that kept other eelers away–was his private fiefdom. And so she must have guessed, just as I had, the letter's location.

I said, "I gather that the Contessa refused to give him the money."

"She did refuse. I had kept a close watch on him that night, because I had feared he would choose the night of the ball to go to her. I saw him come out of the Contessa's room. I had never seen him in such a rage."

"What did he tell you?"

"That the Contessa had refused to give him anything. That instead she had said she would have him arrested for attempted blackmail if he did not go to fetch her lawyer immediately. She was going to change her will. And Emilio could tell all Venice the truth, for all she cared."

Poor Anna, I thought. The Contessa had not really loved her, after all–not for herself. It was only the memory of Antonio that she had loved. And once she knew Anna was not Antonio's child . . .

I asked, "Did Emilio leave the house then?"

"Yes."

But not to fetch the lawyer. Probably he had gone to some café and fueled his rage with brandy. In any case, he had returned sometime later and stabbed the Contessa repeatedly and left her for dead in her wheelchair.

Perhaps he had taken her jewelry because he hoped to realize at least some gain from his muddled enterprise. Or perhaps he wanted to give the impression that the murder had been the work of a professional thief. Anyway, he had taken it. Later, growing frightened, he had planted the jewelry in my room and sent that anonymous note to the police.

Fleetingly I thought of the Constantinople basin. Where

had he hidden that? Well, the police would get that information out of him in time.

I said, "Maria, we had better go now."

"Signorina, what are you going to do with that letter?"

"I'm sorry, Maria, but I must give it to the police. You see that, don't you?"

She said vigorously, "No, signorina, I do not. What good will it do? It will not bring the Contessa back to life. It will only harm Anna."

"Oh, Maria! I don't want to harm Anna. I have grown fond of her, and I know how much you must love her. But she won't be alone, no matter what happens. She will still have you." And perhaps, I thought, now that Maria knew the child did not have Belzoni blood, she would express her love with more than those pitiful, almost furtive caresses she had allowed herself in the past.

"But what neither of us can do," I said, "is to allow the Contessa's murderer to go free. This letter is part of the evidence which will enable the police to arrest him. Don't you see that they must have it?"

She looked at me sorrowfully for a moment, and then bowed her head. "Yes, I see now. I see that nothing I can say will keep you from taking that letter to the police."

"Then shall we go now?"

She stepped back to let me precede her through the doorway.

Perhaps her swift movement made some sound. Or perhaps it was instinct that made me whirl around, to see her with the knife upraised in her right hand, her lips drawn back and her dark eyes bulging.

In the split second before my hand shot up to grasp her right wrist, I thought, "Not Emilio!" It was this determined face, not Emilio's, that my great-aunt must have seen in her last moments of life.

As she tried to wrench her wrist free, I grappled with her,

desperately intent upon twisting that strong wrist until she dropped the knife. For a moment we stood swaying there in the glare and the hot wind, staring into each other's eyes like two madwomen locked in some fantastic dance. Then I felt her instep hook behind my ankle. Before I could prevent it, she had swept my foot out from under me. I went down, still clutching her right wrist, and bringing her tall body down with me.

I lay there panting, right hand shoving against her shoulder, left hand still clamped around her wrist. I thought of pleading with her. But the look on that lined face told me that would be a waste of energy I could not afford. And so instead I gathered all my strength and shoved her away from me.

Rolling to my hands and knees, I started to get to my feet, aware with sudden wild hope that she had been slower than I. She was still on the ground, although half sitting up now, with her left hand pressing into the grass to help her rise. Then, a split second before I could straighten up entirely, she lunged with the knife. I saw sunlight flash along the steel blade, felt it slash through cloth and into the flesh of my upper arm.

The cut was deep. I knew that by the numbing pain, more like that from a sledge hammer blow than a knife slash, that gripped my left arm from shoulder to wrist. No hope now of wresting that knife away. I turned and ran through hot sunlight and the wind-stirred grass. Not toward the skiff. Before I could untie it, she would have plunged the knife into my back. My one chance was that ancient building which someone had used as a stable. If I could get into the loft and draw the ladder up after me, I might have time to reason with her and to stanch the blood I felt flowing down my arm.

I could hear the muffled pound of her footsteps along the path's hard-packed earth. She sounded well behind me, but I dared not look back to make sure. Beginning to feel dizzy, I concentrated upon reaching that ruined building just ahead on the right side of the path.

I ran inside into hot, still dimness broken by patches of sunlight falling through the roof, into smells of mildewed hay and rotting wood. The rickety ladder stood there, its upper end resting against the loft's edge. If I still had the strength to climb it and then draw it up after me . . .

I need not have worried about drawing it up. With my right knee already on the loft floor, I heard a rending sound, felt the rung slant under my left foot, and knew that one of the ladder's side rails had given way. As I threw myself forward to hook my fingers into a crack, I heard the rest of the ladder fall to the earthen floor.

I drew myself onto the loft and then dizzily sat up, facing the door, with my legs curled around me. Maria had come into the shed. She glanced at the useless ladder, and then crossed the packed earth through patches of sunlight to look up at me.

"Maria, help me to get down. Put a tourniquet on my arm and get me to a doctor. If you don't, I'll bleed to death."

"No."

"Please." As I spoke, I was turning back my skirt, ripping off the hem of my petticoat. "I'll give you the letter. No one need ever know about it."

"No. You will tell."

No agitation now in her face or voice. She had the terrible calm of a tigress at the foot of a tree, knowing that sooner or later the human being she has clawed will fall from its branches.

Using one hand, I tried to tie the strip of linen around my blood-soaked arm above the point where the knife had ripped into the cloth. She said, "Don't misunderstand, signorina. I liked you when you first came to Ca' Belzoni. But when Emilio told me about that letter you might have read, I knew I must do something. It is too bad you looked up from the bench that night, signorina. If you had not, you would have died swiftly, and without fear. And it is too bad you chose to run through the fog. I am a strong woman, but I cannot run as fast as you."

I kept fumbling with the length of linen, still unable to tie its ends into a knot. What was she saying? That it was she, not Emilio, who had pried the head loose from the wall and followed me through the fog-shrouded streets two days later? Or was it my increasing lightheadedness that made me think that?

I said, "You can't do this. You can't just stand there and watch—"

"You have not understood me, signorina. Always I have been determined that nothing bad will happen to Anna. When Emilio came out of the Contessa's room and told me what the Contessa had said, I went down to the kitchen and put a knife in my skirt pocket. This knife, signorina."

She held the knife up for a brief moment, and I noticed, with detachment, that there was a red stain on it. Then I fumbled with the tourniquet again. I had a knot now, but I could not pull it tight.

"I went to her room. I pleaded with her, not just for Anna, but for the sake of our friendship—hers and mine. For we were friends, the Contessa and I. I loved her only second to Anna. But when she kept saying that she was going to disown Anna, yes, even if it meant that someday Anna would end up like Rosa, I killed her and took her jewels, so that people would think a common thief had done it."

She broke off. "You mailed the jewels to the police, didn't you, signorina? I did not think you would find them in time to do that."

I made no answer. Answering would have been too much trouble, just as fumbling with the tourniquet was. I sat there and looked at the blood seep from my soaked sleeve down over my hand and onto my lap.

"My life has been hard, signorina. My husband died, my son died before he could grow up, and my daughter—well, we will not speak of her. But Anna is to have a good life. She will grow up in Signore Corsi's house, with his daughters like sisters to her. She will be a fine lady, and someday she will marry a fine gentleman. Nothing is to stop that."

I watched her lay the knife on the upper rail of a stall. Should I again ask her to help me? No, it would be of no use. If she had been a killer-for-gain, she might have spared me, or even a killer-for-revenge. But she killed for the sake of love, and such killers are without mercy.

What was she doing now? For perhaps a minute I watched her gather things—handfuls of hay from the corners of the shed, wood chips from the floor, pieces of broken ladder—and heap them below the loft's edge. Then I understood. She hoped with fire to destroy the evidence of how I had died. Would she leave the island as soon as she had set the fire? My dimming mind fumbled with the question, just as my fingers had struggled with the tourniquet. No, I decided, she would wait out there for a while with her knife to make sure I did not escape from the burning shed.

She had added heavier wood to the pile now—lengths of rail she had wrenched loose from the stall, and what looked like an ancient yoke for oxen. She took a match from her skirt pocket and struck it on the rail where she had placed the knife. Bending, she touched the flame to the straw in several places. Fascinated, I watched little columns of thick white smoke, wavering in the wind, rise from the straw. Then small flames, made pale by sunlight slanting through the roof, burst forth and began to lick at the lighter wood.

She stood quietly, watching the kindling burn and then the heavier wood catch fire, and I watched quietly from the loft. Then she turned, picked up the knife, and left the shed.

The fire burned higher. With faint irritation, as one becomes aware of sound when one is just about to fall asleep, I became aware of the fire's heat, greater than the heat of the sunlight pouring through the broken roof.

A flame shot up with an explosive sound only inches in front of my face. I shrank back.

I think it must have been my own movement, rather than that spurt of flame, which aroused me from my torpor. With my will to live surging back like a tide, I crawled to one side of the loft. Holding to its edge with my right hand, I let myself down. I hung there for a moment, and then dropped.

My ankle turned as I landed, but I felt no pain. Smoke was thick now, and from the hungry roaring of the fire, I knew the loft must have caught. I staggered toward the dimly visible doorway. All my effort, I knew, was buying me only a few additional seconds of life. She would be waiting out there, beyond the smoke and flames, to finish me off. But in every nerve and every ounce of flesh, I was determined to have those additional seconds.

I was through the doorway. Yes, Maria was still out there.

But not standing calmly alert, knife in hand. And not alone. She was struggling in the grasp of a tall figure. I had a blurred impression of another man, a grizzled man in gondolier's clothing, running up the path from the dock.

I called, "Caleb!"

He released Maria and ran toward me. I took a few steps forward, aware as I did so that Maria had darted past me toward the burning shed, and then I sank to my knees.

"Lie down," Caleb said.

I did. Kneeling beside me, he whipped out his pocket handkerchief and twirled it into a thin rope. As he was knotting it around my arm just below the shoulder, I heard him shout, "Francesco! Get that woman out of there!"

He lifted me in his arms and carried me toward the landing stage. I whispered, "Caleb, how—?"

"When I came back to the house and couldn't find you, I went to Anna and bullied her into talking. I told her you might be in great—"

He broke off, quickening his pace. I heard running footsteps behind us. Then I saw the gondolier's appalled face. He said, "I could see her in there, but there's no use trying to get her out."

"Why?"

"She's cut her throat."

I heard my own whimpering cry. Caleb said, "Don't think about it, Sara. Just try to hang on until I can get you to a doctor."

CHAPTER 23

In my brown bombazine traveling costume, and with my packed bag at my feet, I looked at my reflection in the mirror. Even though I had been out of the hospital for a week now, my arm was still in a sling. It did not, I felt, add to my appearance. But at least I had been able to fashion out of an old shawl a brown silk sling to replace the white linen one the hospital had supplied.

I had a sense of the Belzoni house stretching emptily around me. Always the huge marble pile, built to accommodate, not only Belzonis and their hordes of servants, but also Belzoni relatives and guests and *their* servants, had seemed quite empty. Now, though, it was all but deserted. Of the Belzoni family, only Giuseppe was still here. His brother and his sister and her husband, after retaining a legal firm to fight their case, had left Venice–Isabella and Enrico Ponzi for Switzerland, and Carlo for an appearance at Covent Garden in London.

Of the servants, only Hortensia and Louisa and the cook remained. Maria Rugazzi, like the mistress she had murdered, now lay on San Michele Island. Emilio was in jail, awaiting trial for fraud and attempted blackmail. When confronted with the letter I had turned over to the police, he had promptly confessed, probably because he feared a far more grave charge of complicity in the Contessa's murder.

But Anna was here today, for the first time in two weeks.

As soon as Signore Corsi had heard of Maria's death and my hospitalization, he had come with his wife and taken Anna to their house. They had brought her back earlier this afternoon to gather up the rest of her possessions in her room, and to say good-by to me.

And I, of course, was still here. But not for long. Already my trunk had been taken to the *Irelandia,* a cargo-passenger ship anchored off Murano Island.

Someone knocked. Knowing who it must be, I said, "Come in."

Caleb opened the door and then closed it behind him. "Are you ready to leave?"

"Except for saying a last good-by to Anna. Caleb, did you talk to Signore Corsi about the will when he was here this afternoon?"

"Yes. He frankly doesn't know how it will be settled. Because of the statement of that letter-writer in Padua, it is certain now that no court will believe Anna is the Contessa's great-granddaughter."

I nodded. The police had located the man to whom that spurious letter had been dictated. Brought to Venice, he had identified Emilio as the man who had hired his services.

"And yet," Caleb went on, "Anna was legally adopted by the Contessa. Corsi will argue that the adoption is irrevocable, and that therefore Anna has a right to inherit. But all that seems certain, Corsi says, is that the trial will drag on as long as that one in *Bleak House*. And by that time Ca' Belzoni will probably be sold to pay legal fees."

Which would be sad, especially for Giuseppe. But my chief concern was the child who still called me Cousin Sara. "The Corsis still plan to keep Anna, don't they?"

"Oh, yes. Even if the case goes against Anna, he will still regard himself as her guardian."

"I'm glad." I turned back to the mirror. "I hope there aren't any fashionable women on that ship. This dress is so dowdy."

"You could have afforded a new one, if you had allowed me to pay for your passage to New York."

"That was out of the question."

"So you've kept saying. But it's still pretty damn silly, considering that we've arranged for the captain to marry us soon after the *Irelandia* leaves port."

"We are not married yet, Caleb."

He let out a hoot of laughter. Then he drew me to him and, even though he was careful of my arm, managed to kiss me soundly.

"It's going to be fun being married to you, Sara. All those husks of New England rectitude around you. I'm going to peel them off, one by one, until you find you are someone you never dreamed you were."

"I don't think I like the way you put that, Caleb."

But I did like it. Now I liked everything about Caleb. Ever since that day I had almost died in that loft on Santa Theodosia, I had been eager for life. And Caleb, besides being the man I loved, was the most alive man I would be apt to encounter.

And he was right about those husks. There was another Sara Randall inside them. The day I had seen the boy with the dolphin, I had caught a glimpse of that other Sara, a young woman capable of more heady joy than some people might consider wise or even proper.

He said, picking up my valise, "Well, let's say good-by to Anna."

"Wait! Where's your valise?"

"I sent it to the ship, along with your trunk."

We went to Anna's room. Despite the two tragic losses she had suffered, she looked less pale than she had when I first came to this house, and her smile was more spontaneous and childlike. It was good for her to be in the Corsi house, and with the Corsi children. Whether or not the Belzoni fortune was ultimately awarded to her, she had a better chance now for that good life her grandmother had been so fanatically determined for her to have.

"Did you and Louisa get everything packed?" I looked at her small leather trunk at the foot of the bed. "The Corsis will be back here for you at three, you know."

"We put everything in the trunk except Paco's things."

"Then I'll say good-by to you, Anna." I bent and kissed her.

"Good-by, Cousin Sara." Her face was wistful, but not as much so as it would have been two weeks before. She had a mother and father now, and two sisters.

I looked around the room. "I suppose I had better say good-by to Paco, too. Where is Paco?"

At the sound of his name, Paco hurtled off the top of the wardrobe. But not at me—at the tallest objective in the room, Caleb. The monkey landed, chattering, on his chest and wrapped small arms around Caleb's head. Face buried in monkey fur, Caleb took a reeling step or two, shouting in a muffled voice and trying to pry Paco loose.

Caleb's foot struck some object that gave forth a muffled, metallic sound. Paco let go then and leaped, still chattering, to the headboard of Anna's small bed.

Caleb and I stared down at Paco's water dish, hand-crafted by his young mistress. A piece of it had fallen away, revealing yellow metal set with a red stone. Bending, Caleb picked up the dish and, with thumb and forefinger, broke off another piece of reddish clay. A topaz gleamed at me in the afternoon light.

Looking at me, Caleb asked, "The Constantinople basin?"

I nodded, unable to speak.

He laid it on the dressing table. Then we both turned to Anna.

It was because of something Giuseppe had said, she told us, that she had done it. He had come to the Contessa's room one afternoon and seen Anna sitting with the basin in her lap.

He had told his grandmother that she might "come to harm" if she persisted in keeping that basin in her room.

"I didn't want that to happen, so I waited until she fell asleep. Always before, I put the basin behind her dressing table, but that day I brought it here and put clay around it. It was almost time for me to make Paco a new water dish, anyway."

Caleb and I stared at each other in dumfounded silence. Then, simultaneously, we burst out laughing. "It's probably the first time in a thousand years," Caleb said, "that that thing has been put to practical use. Give it to Signore Corsi to keep for the estate, Anna. And tell Giuseppe that story. We may not have time to."

We left her then and went in search of Giuseppe. We found him in the grand salon, sketching the nuptial chariot that raced across the ceiling. He shook our hands in farewell and then said to me, "You look beautiful, Sara. Happiness becomes you. But you really should do something about that traveling costume." He turned to Caleb. "Couldn't you have persuaded her to buy a new one?"

"You don't understand, Giuseppe. That dress represents New England virtue. In mid-Atlantic I shall throw it overboard, along with a few other husks."

"Caleb!"

We went to the ground floor then and shook hands with the cook and Hortensia and Louisa. Then we went out the Grand Canal entrance and moved along the walkway toward the public landing stage. Caleb said, "Well, I guess we've said all our good-bys."

"Not quite. Caleb, do we have time to go a little way down the side canal, and then circle back?"

"Of course, sweetheart. But why?"

"There's someone else I want to say good-by to before we leave Venice. A little boy on a bridge. He isn't alive. He's bronze, and he's hugging a dolphin."